P9-ELS-333

Song of the Shaggy Canary

Westminster Press Books by
PHYLLIS ANDERSON WOOD

Song of the Shaggy Canary
I've Missed a Sunset or Three
Your Bird Is Here, Tom Thompson
Andy

Song of the Shaggy Canary

by

PHYLLIS ANDERSON WOOD

THE WESTMINSTER PRESS
Philadelphia

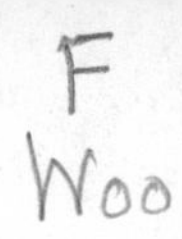

BOOK DESIGN BY
DOROTHY ALDEN SMITH

Published by The Westminster Press®
Philadelphia, Pennsylvania

PRINTED IN THE UNITED STATES OF AMERICA

Library of Congress Cataloging in Publication Data

Wood, Phyllis Anderson.
Song of the shaggy canary.

SUMMARY: An eighteen-year-old divorcee with a baby and a young veteran hurt by the war and a broken engagement want friendship without commitment, but find themselves becoming committed to each other.
I. Title.
PZ7.W854So [Fic] 73–14785
ISBN 0–664–32543–2

To Stephen Wood
whose advice on my manuscripts
I value highly

Contents

Summer's End

I RECOGNIZED JOHN NOLAN INSTANTLY AS HE OPENED the front door of Hoover High and slowly stepped into the main corridor. Glancing around to be sure he was alone, he went over to a bronze wall plaque and ran his finger down the list of Hoover students in the Armed Forces.

Near the end of the column his moving hand stopped. His tall frame slumped and for a moment he leaned against the plaque, his head resting on his upraised arm. John had no idea I was watching through the glass office door.

Although I hadn't known him personally, I clearly remembered how John Nolan's easygoing manner had made him one of the most popular juniors at Hoover High. But that was two years ago. Now he looked tired and sad.

John waited a few minutes by the plaque and then turned toward the office where I was working at the counter. When he paused at the door, a ninth-grader crowded past him and darted through the opening. John shook his head and approached the counter.

"Are they all that small now?" he asked.

"They grow up sooner or later," I said. "You did."

He looked at me uneasily. I could see him searching around in his memory.

"Sandra Martin," I said, helping him out. "We had an art class together."

He didn't react.

"I was a sophomore," I added. "You were a junior."

"I'm afraid I don't remember you," he said. "But I'm John Nolan."

He studied my face carefully for a moment.

"Now I do remember a little. You sat over by the window. You never talked to anyone but that curly-haired kid."

"Now you remember," I agreed.

He stood at the counter, studying everything around the office.

"What brings you back?" I asked.

He shook his head quickly as if to brush off the old memories.

"Oh . . . I came back to get my records sent to the adult school. I'm going to finish at night."

"All right," I answered, reaching for the transcript request form. "You just fill out this top part and sign at the bottom of the page. We do the rest."

A trace of a smile crossed his face, but it passed quickly. The sad look returned.

"Okay," he said, handing back the completed form. "Will it take very long?"

"We'll get it right out," I assured him.

"Thanks," he said as he went out the door.

He passed the Armed Forces list in the hallway and paused again.

"Wow! Who was that ray of sunshine?" asked Peggy, the secretary.

"The dream man of the junior class two years ago," I answered. "He was going steady with Linda Campbell."

"So what's dream man doing going to night school?" Peggy wondered.

"I think he joined the service at the end of his junior year. He dropped out of sight," I recalled.

While I was wondering what had happened in those two years to change the relaxed and pleasant John Nolan into a young man who put people off, suddenly he stood before me at the counter again.

"If you were a sophomore when I was a junior," he said, "then how come you're still in school two years later? You don't look that dumb."

My mind flashed painfully back over two years filled with a dreamy Christmas wedding during my junior year, a young husband who took off three months later when he learned I was pregnant, a lonely divorce, and a young son, Chuckie, who was the only joy left over from the whole dreary scene.

There was no way I could fill him in on those two years.

"I can be pretty dumb," I answered. "Unbelievably dumb."

"Can't we all," he said. "Can't we all . . ."

With that he turned and started to leave. At the doorway he glanced back briefly.

"Anyhow, it's been good seeing you again," he said as he went out the door.

"Funny," I commented to Peggy, "for just a fleeting moment that was the old John Nolan—the one who left people feeling good."

I busied myself at the counter, checking his transcript form.

So much for John Nolan, I said to myself as I filed his request in the urgent basket.

HAVING PUT JOHN OUT OF MY MIND, I TURNED MY attention to the changeover that always took place when the closing bell rang.

At three o'clock each day I was like an actor switching roles between scenes. I left school as a seventeen-year-old senior and arrived at my tiny apartment as the mother of a ten-month-old baby.

"I know you're tired, Mom. I'll take over now," I said as I came through the front door and started pushing Chuckie's portable crib into the bedroom.

"I'll just get things organized for your dinner and then run on home, dear."

"Thanks, Mom."

I flopped on my bed with Chuckie beside me. As he played happily with his toes I found myself wondering what John Nolan would think if he could see me at home . . . the girl who sat over by the window in art and never talked to anyone except that curly-haired kid. What a spoiled baby that handsome curly-haired kid had turned out to be when he was my husband for three miserable months!

"So . . . we don't need anyone but ourselves, do we, Chuckie?" I said to the warm, little baby snuggled against me. "We'll manage alone."

While he was quiet and contented I picked up my history book and started the homework assignment. I had just reached the War of 1812 when my mother's voice interrupted my reading.

"Sandy, did you bring home some baby food and milk?"

"I completely forgot," I called. "I'll go to the market in just a moment."

Turning to Chuckie, I made a bargain.

"If you'll be a quiet baby for ten more minutes while I finish this chapter, we'll go out for a walk. Okay?" He seemed to agree for once and let me reach a stopping place.

The minute I got out his little blue jacket and zipped him into it, Chuckie sensed that fun things were about to happen. He loved riding in the stroller and always made cheerful noises as he traveled.

I was so absorbed in counting my money and figuring how much baby food I could afford to buy that I hardly noticed the figure coming from behind and catching up to walk beside me.

"We meet again," John Nolan said as he slowed his pace to mine.

"Oh . . . hi."

I made my answer sound casual on purpose. John looked like someone with too many problems for me. I had enough of my own.

"Where are you headed?" he asked.

"Just to the market."

We walked along in silence except for the squeaky wheel on Chuckie's stroller.

"Doesn't that stroller wheel bother you?" he asked.

"It didn't until you mentioned it," I said. "Now it might drive me crazy."

"Is this where you're shopping?" John asked as we approached the supermarket. "I have to find something I can cook on the hot plate in my room. My meals . . ." He shook his head. "It might be healthier to starve to death."

"Well, good luck on the dinner," I said as I headed down the baby food aisle.

"Hey," he called, "I'll put some oil on that wheel as you go past my place. Meet me at the check-out counter when you're finished."

He must be kidding, I thought. Nobody worries about such little things. But his manner seemed completely serious.

"Okay," I agreed.

"Did you find anything good for your dinner?" I asked as John came through the check-out counter and we started toward home.

"Hot dogs, potato chips, chocolate milk, and apples," he said, looking into his bag to be sure.

"I see what you mean about your meals."

John almost smiled for a moment.

"I'd offer to share," I said, "if you'd prefer strained squash, applesauce, chopped beef, and vanilla pudding."

"You're worse off than I am with that stuff," he commented.

"Oh, I was only shopping for Chuckie," I explained. "Things aren't all that bad."

As we walked along John glared at the squeaky stroller wheel. Then he bent over and looked into Chuckie's laughing face.

"I really don't know if I should take that squeak away from him," he said doubtfully. "He seems to like it."

Again he almost smiled, but caught himself in time.

I was amused because I knew that Chuckie laughed at anything and everything when he was out in the stroller.

"Do you baby-sit with him every day?" John asked.

I took a deep breath and wondered how to answer that one. It was a long story, and I didn't feel ready to tell it to John Nolan or anyone.

"Yes," I said. "Every day."

John dropped the subject.

"What have *you* done in these last two years?" I asked.

"The service," John answered. From his tone I knew the subject was closed. He wasn't about to expose his private world either.

We walked along without talking. Then, pointing

to a rooming house, John eased the stroller off the curb and pushed it across the street.

"My room is up there. I'll get the oil and be right down," he said.

I was still recovering from the shock of having someone help me get the stroller across a street when John returned and busied himself with the wheel.

"There you are," he said as he straightened up his tall frame. "No squeak to drive you crazy now."

"I'll have to find something else, I guess."

John only shook his head.

"Thank you," I added. "It was nice of you to worry about it for me."

He shrugged his shoulders.

"I have to hurry," I said, not waiting to see if he'd say more. "Chuckie is getting hungry—and that won't wait."

"See you around," he answered.

IT WAS A BUSY WEEK WITH CHUCKIE AND SCHOOL AND housework. John Nolan didn't even cross my mind until the following Monday.

I was shopping in the drugstore when I noticed three of the girls who had been a year ahead of me in school huddled together talking about their jobs. Feeling a little envious, I moved closer to listen in on their talk. Their lives were completely different from mine. And then I caught a familiar name.

"Has anyone seen John Nolan since he got back?"

"I've seen him, but a lot of good it did me! He sort of nodded in recognition and didn't even stop to speak."

"I hear that's what he's been doing to everybody. I haven't heard of a single person that he's even spoken to since he got back."

"Well, after the way he got burned by Linda I can see why he'd be pretty cautious with people."

"Yeah, that was some deal she gave him—hounding him until he finally bought her an engagement ring, and then the very night he left for the service going out with someone else."

"It's a good thing she finally wrote and broke their engagement . . . but John probably took it hard. That's not the way he does things."

"And besides that, I heard that John's best friend was killed in an auto accident at just about the same time."

By then I had read all the labels near me and there was no other excuse for standing there in the aisle. I had already heard enough to make me start looking at John in a different light.

I paid and left the store, thinking about John eating his hot dogs, potato chips, and apples alone in his room. Even if he is serious and sad, I thought, he did notice my need. He wanted to help.

I don't think the girls know much about him, I concluded.

And what are you, I asked myself, a psychiatrist or something? He oils your stroller wheel and suddenly you know what's going on inside him?

Besides, I thought with a note of caution, what does it matter anyway? You'd better give your attention to Chuckie. Forget it.

THE PASSING PERIOD BETWEEN CLASSES OFTEN BROUGHT a flood of impatient people into the office. We were caught up in one of those waves a few days later, with kids piled up four deep at the counter. Everyone was going to be late for a class, everyone had to have something signed, everyone was demanding attention. Everyone, that is, except a quiet figure in the background.

I don't know when John Nolan had entered the office, but I spotted him through the crowd standing against the wall—out of the way. Remembering his businesslike manner in the office the first time, I wondered if he might resent being kept waiting.

"Just a minute, kids," I said to the crowd in front of me.

Ignoring my request, they continued to push for attention.

"Mr. Nolan," I called over their heads, "I'll help you now if you're in a hurry."

John shook his head. "It can wait. Go ahead and finish there."

Finally the crowd cleared out and the office was quiet again. John stepped up to the counter.

"I'm sorry you had to wait so long," I apologized.

"You really had your hands full," he said.

"Oh, I'm getting used to juggling everybody's

needs and demands—at school, at home, everywhere. Sometimes I feel like a piece of elastic being stretched and pulled in both directions."

"I know the feeling," he said.

Suddenly I was embarrassed to have gotten so personal when I was tending the counter.

"I stopped in to check on my transcript," John said, tactfully bringing me back to business. "I have an appointment this evening with the adult school counselor, and I wanted to be sure he'd have my records when I got there. It's pretty important to me."

"Let me check for you," I said, opening the file. "Yes, it was sent out in the district mail the same day you requested it."

"By the way, do you know anything about these night school classes?" he asked as he pulled the adult school schedule from his pocket.

"Almost nothing," I admitted, "but maybe we can find some answers."

He was scanning the list. I was reading it upside down across the counter. My eye stopped at one class—SEWING FOR CHILDREN. A quick vision of Chuckie in a little red outfit, made by me, flashed through my mind.

"Here's one I wanted to ask about," John said.

After a moment I felt his eyes on me . . . waiting.

"Oh, I'm sorry. What did you say?"

"I lost you. Where did you get off?"

"At the class called SEWING FOR CHILDREN. I'd love to take that."

"You have to be eighteen to enroll for evening classes in this district, don't you?" he asked. "You're not, are you?"

"Well, almost," I said, hesitating.

"Sandy," Peggy chimed in helpfully, "I think you can get into an adult class as the head of a family, regardless of age."

John shot a startled glance at me. I wanted to melt into a puddle and soak into the floor. My whole dreary story was being revealed to John in the worst possible way at the worst possible time. How would I answer the next question?

The next question made me appreciate John Nolan. He changed the subject.

"Do you want to try it?" he asked. "Classes start tonight. The one you want meets Mondays and Wednesdays."

"I couldn't on such short notice," I said.

A quick flash of wistfulness over my lost freedom tarnished my shiny new dream. I couldn't even sign up for a class without arranging baby-sitting for Chuckie.

"I could go by the room tonight and ask if there's space in the class for you—if you could get there by Wednesday," he suggested. "Shall I do that?"

What a nice person, I thought to myself. And the girls in the drugstore said he puts people off.

"I would appreciate that," I said. I hoped he would sense how deeply I was touched.

My desire to go to a night school class stirred up a whole new set of problems. But the more I thought about the problems, the more I wanted the class. I had reached a point in my life where I had to find out if there were ways I could do things and still be a good mother.

Up until now baby-sitting had never been an issue. Since my social life had amounted to zero after my marriage and divorce, I had never needed any baby-sitting except for school hours—and my mother handled this as her contribution toward getting me self-supporting.

Now suddenly there was an adult activity I wanted to be part of, and I couldn't ask my mother how to manage it. She would have felt that I was hinting for her to do more.

I had no friends with babies whom I could ask. The only person near us with a small child was the woman in the house next door. She had three grown boys and a little toddler. We had never become acquainted, but she always seemed pleasant with her family.

When Chuckie was asleep I decided to slip out and go next door for a moment.

I stood uncomfortably on the neighbors' porch waiting for someone to answer my knock. When the door opened I was met by a small boy wearing nothing but underpants and a broad smile.

"Is your mother home?" I asked.

He stood there, still smiling.

"Where's your mommy?" I asked, stooping down to his level.

He smiled.

Just then his surprised mother walked past the door.

"Oh," she gasped, "I didn't hear the doorbell. And I didn't know Georgie had opened the door. I was running the bath water."

"I'm Sandy Martin," I said. "I live next door."

"Of course. I've seen you with your baby. I'm Edith Klopman. Come in, won't you?"

"Well, I know you're busy right now, but I was hoping maybe you could tell me how it's done . . . getting baby-sitters, I mean."

"It's a problem. It's hard to find dependable sitters and it costs so much that sometimes it hardly seems worth going out. What kind of sitting did you need?"

"I want to take a night school class on Mondays and Wednesdays."

Mrs. Klopman thought for a moment. "We might work out a deal that wouldn't take money," she suggested. Then she stopped to think again. "Could you put Chuckie to bed over here on those two evenings and take Georgie on two afternoons while I shop and do errands?"

"Oh, I could manage that," I assured her. "Would you really want to do that?"

"Yes," she agreed after a moment's hesitation. "I've watched you with your baby. I would trust you with Georgie. When do classes start?"

"Tonight," I said, "but I think I'll be able to enroll at the second class."

"We'll plan definitely on Wednesday, then?" Mrs. Klopman asked.

"Great," I answered, patting Georgie's head as he stood there in his underpants feeling perfectly dressed for visitors. "I was afraid I wouldn't be able to work out anything. This is wonderful."

"I think we'll both enjoy some freedom," she said with a warm smile.

I hurried back to Chuckie. He hadn't stirred in his crib.

"You're a lovely baby," I said to him, "but you certainly do make life complicated." He seemed untroubled by this thought. "By the way," I added, "would you care to have some new clothes . . . made by your mother, no less?"

Later in the evening, as I realized how much my hopes were set on getting into that sewing class, I had a chilling thought. What if John Nolan had only been making polite conversation? Maybe he would forget about the sewing class. Or maybe he would be embarrassed to go in when he saw all the women in the class. Or maybe the class would be full. And I'd be all dressed up in my hopes and plans with no place to go.

It seemed pretty strange for someone to sit through high school classes in American history,

English lit, and typing, worrying all the while about getting into an adult class called SEWING FOR CHILDREN. But that's just how mixed up my life was.

The more I thought about the sewing class, the more remote my chances seemed. I began to prepare myself for disappointment. After all, John Nolan didn't even know where I lived. In order to tell me about the class he would have to come back to school while I was working in the office. And maybe he couldn't—he might have a daytime job. I could see that it just wasn't going to work out.

Trying to live with my disappointment, I hurried into the office right after lunch to work at the counter.

"There's a message for you on my desk," Peggy called from the back office. "Mr. Sunshine left it for you."

"Let's not make fun of him," I said softly. "He's nice, and he's had some problems."

"Sorry," Peggy said.

Nervously I opened the envelope and pulled out a mimeographed sheet. A note was scrawled across the top of the page: "Class enrollment limited to twenty students. I got you on the list as #20. Call me at 629–4545 if you still want to go."

"Yippee!" I yelled. "He did it. I'm in."

"What did he do and what are you in?" Peggy asked.

"I'm going to get to take the evening class."

"This is such a big deal—to take a class after a day of school?"

"It is if you haven't been anywhere for ten months without taking a baby along."

"I'm glad for you, Sandy. I think it's a wonderful idea."

I was studying the sheet John had left me. It was a list of equipment needed for the class, along with suggested patterns and fabrics. The little red outfit appeared again in my mind.

It was exciting, having something to look forward to—something I was doing by choice, not by necessity. It occurred to me that I was feeling some enthusiasm for the first time in a long, long while.

Finally the school day was over and I hurried home to tell the good news to my mother. As I walked I was furiously figuring what I could get along without in order to buy the sewing materials.

My mother listened to the plan and with a smile went to her purse and took out some money.

"Here, I want to finance the first garment to be made for my grandson by his mother."

"No, Mom," I argued, "you already do so much for us."

"Go on out now and select something that you think is perfect to work on. I'm delighted that you're finally going to have some social activity. I've been worried about your carrying such heavy responsibilities when you're so young . . . so little fun in your life."

"I just don't know how Chuckie and I would make it if you weren't so good to us, Mom."

"That's what families are for, Sandy—to stick together. Hurry now," she urged. "I'll start your dinner while you have some fun shopping."

"Thanks, Mom," I said as I zipped Chuckie into his jacket. "Come on, little one. You'll have to show me what you like."

AN HOUR LATER I PAUSED BEFORE PUSHING THE stroller out through the door of the fabric shop. Chuckie was getting restless after the long wait in the store. It was close to his dinner time.

I tucked my package of sewing things into the stroller beside him. He squirmed around and fussed a little until he discovered the funny sound the paper bag would make if he crunched it in his fingers.

Relieved that he had found something to play with, I looked out of the glass doors while I buttoned my coat. When I turned back to Chuckie he was busily chewing up a mouthful of paper bag.

"Oh, come on, little boy," I said as I fished it out of his mouth, "people don't eat bags!"

This started him crying and I knew it was the beginning of his breaking-up process. He had been good as long as he could.

I brought a little bag of graham crackers out of my purse—just enough to keep him busy till we got home. Chuckie calmed down and I pushed the stroller out into the open air.

I stopped and took a deep breath. Evening was almost on us. The western sky was taking on a rosy glow. The air was crisp and fresh. Something was different.

Do you know, I said to myself, that you haven't taken a real deep breath like that for months? You have forgotten how it feels to stand up straight and look around at the world. Ever since you were left to face a pregnancy and a baby alone you've been tied together with string to keep yourself from falling apart. You've been living and breathing all rolled up in a tight little knot.

It didn't seem as if some little night school class could be so world-shaking. But actually it did mark the beginning of my being able to be a bit of a person as well as somebody's mother.

Racing against Chuckie's hunger, I hurried home, just as I had rushed often before. This time the quick walk was invigorating instead of tiring, and I found myself humming a popular tune that had been going around in my head all day.

John will be going to his evening class tonight, I thought. If I don't hurry, I won't be able to catch him with a phone call. I quickened my steps even more until I was almost running.

"Sandy! You look so young and alive," my mother gasped as I opened the front door. "Your cheeks are rosy like they used to be when you played out in the cold."

"Do you think you could watch Chuckie for just a minute, Mom, while I make a call about the evening class? If I don't call now, I might miss him."

"Sure," she agreed as she helped Chuckie out of

his jacket. Suddenly she looked up in surprise. "You might miss *him?* Is that what you said?"

"Don't get any ideas, Mom. It's just a 'somebody to talk to' type of deal."

"Well, I'm glad. You certainly do need somebody to talk to besides a baby and a mother. I'll start giving Chuckie his dinner; you go ahead and make your call."

Nervously I dialed the number John had written on the sewing sheet. Answer . . . please answer . . ., I said to myself as I listened to the phone ringing in his room. When he did answer I didn't know how to begin.

"John?"

"Hi, Sandy."

"I managed to get it all arranged. I can go to the sewing class."

"Good. I've discovered that night classes aren't all that bad. I hope you'll enjoy yours too."

"I plan to. And I appreciate your getting me onto the class list before it closed."

"It wasn't too hard, except I felt a little silly signing a class list with all those ladies sitting there."

"Did they laugh at you?"

"Oh, no, they were a friendly group—mostly grandmothers, probably."

"Nobody young?" I asked, feeling uneasy. "Will I fit in all right?"

"Why not?"

For a moment there was silence.

"By the way," he added, "I don't have a car yet, but do you want me to walk over with you, Sandy?"

"I'd be glad if you would."

"Okay," he agreed, "six thirty."

"Fine."

Feeling relieved and happy, I put the phone down. It was all happening. I'm going to be me, I thought. On Monday and Wednesday evenings I'm going to be me! Suddenly it dawned on me that I hadn't given John my address.

Quickly I dialed his number. He answered promptly.

"Sandy?"

"Yes. Are you wondering about my scrambled brains?"

"A little."

I gave him my address and explained that I might be next door putting Chuckie to bed at Mrs. Klopman's when he came.

With that arranged, I went in to Chuckie. Giving him a hug, I settled down to feed him his dinner. Remarkably, he seemed to eat more neatly. He smiled a lot more. In fact, he had become a very handsome child, I decided.

BY THE TIME JOHN ARRIVED ON WEDNESDAY, CHUCKIE was at Mrs. Klopman's and I was uneasy with my new freedom. As we started walking toward school in the brisk night air, I took a deep breath. It came out sounding like a sigh . . . and it felt wonderful.

"Tired?" John asked.

"Just beginning to unwind," I explained. "It's the first time I've left Chuckie with anyone but my mother."

I could feel John glance over at me. We walked along in silence.

"He is your baby, isn't he?" John asked uncertainly.

"He's definitely my baby."

"Do you want to talk about it or not?"

"Well, it's been such a mess . . . I haven't wanted to talk at all."

"You don't have to."

"I'd rather have you know it straight, I think."

John glanced over again. "Did some guy go off and leave you to have a baby alone?"

"Oh, it's better than that. My *husband* took off and left me to have our baby alone."

"You're kidding."

"I wish I were."

"You were married and he left you when you got pregnant?"

"Yeah. How's that for a neat honeymoon?"

John looked stunned.

"Chuckie is the only good thing to come out of a bad two years," I added. "He's all I have."

"Who was the guy?"

"Would you believe . . . the curly-haired kid I sat by in art?"

John took a long time to answer. "I wonder how he likes himself now."

"I know how his parents like him now! They're nice people. They even pay as much child support as they can. Without them and my mother I'd be in real trouble."

"I'm glad you told me, Sandy. I could tell you were different from the other girls I used to know, but I didn't know how different."

"By the way," I said, bringing the conversation back to John, "I heard some talk about your having gotten a raw deal too."

I hoped I wasn't bringing up a painful subject too soon.

"Yeah, Linda broke our engagement while I was stationed overseas."

"That would be hard to take," I said.

"I can live with it," he answered.

Then John looked directly at me and said, "I think that's why I feel comfortable with you, Sandy. We've both had it—the promises and the mess of broken promises."

"That about sums it up," I agreed.

THE CLASS WAS JUST AS PLEASANT AS I HAD HOPED IT would be. John was right—most of the women were grandmothers, kind ladies who brought me into their conversations at the sewing table.

"Did you have a good time?" John asked when class was over.

"Uh-huh," I said happily. "How was your class?"

"Good. Better than the history class I had in day school."

"How long will it take to earn your diploma?"

"Possibly a year. But the counselor says I might be able to cut it down to just a few basic requirements if I can pass the equivalency exams for all the elective credits."

"That sounds hopeful."

"It does. I'm in a hurry now to get into junior college and start becoming somebody."

"You're somebody now."

"Well, somebody maybe—but I have to be something too." As John touched on the subject of his future, his eyes had a faraway look.

"What are you going to be?"

"The only thing I know is what I learned from my time in the service—that I can't stand to be part of any more tearing down and breaking up. . . . I have to be in some work where I can put broken pieces back together. Otherwise I won't be able to stand life."

"You know, that's the way I feel sometimes."

We were so comfortable together that I was glad I had leveled with John.

"How will you handle Chuckie?" he asked as we reached my place.

"He's a sound sleeper, so I probably can just pick

him up in his blankets and carry him home to his crib."

"Is there other stuff to carry too?"

"With a baby there's a load wherever you go!"

"Then I'll stop and help."

"You're too good to be true."

John smiled briefly and followed me up Mrs. Klopman's steps.

In the darkened bedroom, while Chuckie slept soundly, I packed the bag with the extra diapers, bottles, and spare blanket, and topped it all off with a teddy bear.

As John took the bag from my hand I leaned over the crib to pick up my sleeping baby. Without warning all my feelings rushed to the surface. Tears started to roll down my cheeks and soak into Chuckie's blanket. They wouldn't stop. All I could do was lean on the crib and sob.

"What's the matter, Sandy?" John asked in a quiet voice. He sounded worried.

I shook my head and kept on crying.

"Sandy?" He lifted my chin gently. "What is it? Tell me."

"I don't know what it is, John . . . not really. It's just . . . I guess . . . I don't know. When you helped me just then . . . it all came to me. . . . I've had . . . a baby . . . for ten months . . . and . . . and . . . not once . . . not once in that baby's life . . . not once . . . has a man been around to help . . . with one single thing."

John looked at me but said nothing. I was struggling for control. I swallowed the final sob and lifted Chuckie from his crib. Wiping my eyes on a corner of his blanket, I wrapped him up snugly and held him close. Together we tiptoed out, waving a silent thanks to Mrs. Klopman as she held the front door open for us.

"The apartment key is in my left pocket," I whispered as we approached my steps.

John found it and quietly opened the door.

"Don't leave," I said softly as I hurried to the bedroom to put my sleeping baby into his own crib. Chuckie melted into a relaxed sleeping position and didn't stir. I covered him, patted his back, and tiptoed out. John was still standing in the hall by the front door.

"Thank you very much, John," I said as I took the bag he was still holding. "Do you want some hot chocolate or something?"

"Not tonight, thanks. I'd better be getting along. I have to take the first of the equivalency exams in the morning."

"Thanks again, then."

"I'll be by next Monday . . . same time . . . okay?"

"Fine," I agreed.

DURING THE WEEK, AS I WENT ABOUT MY BUSINESS, John occasionally came into my mind. He was something of a puzzle to me. It was almost as if he were two different persons—one burdened by a sadness, standing apart from people as if he didn't want anyone to know he was hurting; the other, warm and caring.

Since I had seen his warm side most recently when he helped get Chuckie home from Mrs. Klopman's, it was a surprise to see the very serious John Nolan waiting on my doorstep Monday evening.

"Anything wrong?" I asked as we started walking.

"No."

There was an uncomfortable silence. A wall was between us.

"Something's on your mind. Want to talk about it?" I asked.

"I'm afraid you'll take it wrong," he said.

"You could try me," I suggested. "I've been kicked a few times. Whatever you have to say can't be as bad as some of the choice things my husband said."

"Who wants to try to beat his record?" John asked, sounding hurt.

"I just meant that I could take whatever you might have to say."

"Well, the problem is—I've decided I want to be completely honest in my relationship with you, Sandy. You're too nice a person for me to lead on."

"Lead on to what?" I asked, flaring up unexpectedly. "What could you be leading me into? If I can be responsible for a baby, I guess I can be responsible for myself. Nobody's—"

"Hold it, Sandy. Slow down. I said I was afraid you'd take it wrong. Forget it."

He quickened his steps and moved on ahead of me.

"Try again. Please?" I begged as I hurried to catch up. "I promise . . . no more outbursts."

"You really want to know what's on my mind, Sandy?"

I nodded.

"Well . . . you've been through a lot, and I've had a few blows . . . and I think we can be friends because of this."

Again I nodded.

"I would like to have you as a friend. But I want you to know in advance that it's going to have to be a 'no strings attached' friendship. I definitely do not want anyone trying to own me."

He seemed to be making this final pronouncement more to himself than to me. Then he stopped and looked squarely at me.

Suddenly I felt fine. All of this was leading up to what sounded good to me—friendship and freedom.

"If you only knew how much I don't want to go through all that hassle again, you'd feel very safe with me," I assured him. "I'm already tied to a man. A very young man. Ten months old. What I need is an adult friend, preferably someone who goes to night school too."

The wall was down. John flashed a quick smile of relief as we walked toward the steps of the school.

AT NINE FIFTEEN ONE OF THE WOMEN AT MY SEWING table leaned over to get my attention. "I think there's a young man outside the door trying to contact you, dear."

I turned around to look out the door. Poor John was trying to hide from the class and still get through to me. I hurried out to him.

"I'll be at the counseling office," he said in a low voice. "Do you want to come on down when your class lets out? I didn't want you standing around here wondering why I didn't come."

"Okay. I'll meet you there."

As I watched his tall, lean frame move away down the hall, I thought how much I didn't know about that man.

"Your husband?" the lady next to me asked as I returned to my table.

"Just a friend," I explained.

"Such a kind-looking young man," she murmured.

I smiled and finished up my sewing.

The night school office was something new. As I sat there, waiting for John, every teacher who passed by smiled or made some friendly comment. When I worked at the Hoover counter I often thought that a person might sit there and die, and nobody would ask, "Is anything wrong?"

When the counselor appeared at the door of his office, still talking to John, he glanced up and smiled at me. After shaking hands with John, he asked, "Do you need help, young lady?"

"Not with night school," I said, laughing. "It seems to be the only thing I do that is simple and fun."

"I'd be out of business if they all felt that way," the counselor said.

I could tell from John's face that he had just heard something that pleased him.

"Good news?" I asked as we headed down the street.

"Unbelievable. I passed all five equivalency exams and they earned me fifty credits. I only have to finish up the required subjects I'm taking right now and I'll have my diploma."

"By Christmas," I said. "What a present!"

"It means I can enroll for the spring semester at Fairview and get started on some training that will make me useful."

"Do you know what it will be?"

"No. I've been too busy starving to give much attention to that problem. Now that the exams are off my hands, I have to start looking for a daytime job. My GI entitlement isn't enough to keep me going indefinitely."

We talked about job possibilities as we walked home.

"With jobs so hard to get these days," John concluded, "you almost have to know someone who is leaving a position and be there as he walks out the door."

"I hope you meet someone going out a door . . . soon," I whispered as John opened the apartment door so I could carry Chuckie into his crib.

With a quick silent wave, he turned and hurried down the steps.

"Wednesday," he called back.

I smiled.

In order to be free on my two class nights, I cared for Georgie Klopman on Tuesday and Thursday afternoons. It wasn't bad, really. Georgie was three, and Chuckie thought he was fun.

When I arrived to pick up Georgie on the next Tuesday, Mrs. Klopman was ready to go out.

"I'm going to take a new robe over to my aunt at Hill Haven," she said.

I looked at the warm sunshine and thought how pleasant it would be to walk with the children instead of staying in the house.

"Is she in the nursing home on Millwood Avenue?" I asked.

"Yes."

"We could walk down with it and save you the trip," I suggested. "Georgie is a good walker and Chuckie will go anywhere his stroller takes him."

"I don't want to impose on you, Sandy."

"No trouble. On a day like this we'd like to be out. Want to go walking, boys?"

Georgie grinned. Then he leaned over and made Chuckie nod his head too.

"If the kids want to walk and you don't feel it's a

hardship, I'd really appreciate your taking it, Sandy. I do have a lot to do today."

Mrs. Klopman gave us her aunt's name and room number and we started off toward Millwood Avenue. Our route took us past John's rooming house, but I figured he would be out job-hunting somewhere.

Just after we had passed his place I heard John calling to me. He was hanging out of his second-story window.

"Sandy, wait. . . . I'll be right down," he said.

Within seconds he was standing beside us.

"This is Mrs. Klopman's son," I explained as he looked questioningly at Georgie. "He's my ticket to night school, you know."

"Where are you headed?" John asked, eyeing my bundle.

"To deliver a robe to a patient at Hill Haven on Millwood. It's Georgie's great-aunt."

"I've been job-hunting all day—unsuccessfully. Could I walk along, too?"

"Of course," I agreed. "Tell me about the job-hunting on the way."

As we walked John told about all the places he had tried for positions. It was the same story at each place . . . too many good men applying for each job, even the unskilled and low-paying ones. He was very discouraged.

As we passed an empty lot Georgie spotted some blooming flowers and stopped to pick a handful. He gathered a lot of bent stems and stemless blossoms, but he clutched his bouquet lovingly.

"For Mamma," he said.

"She'll like them," I assured him as we turned into the driveway of Hill Haven.

"I'll wait here for you," John said as he sank into a chair in the lobby. "I'm just a tagalong on this mission."

The lady at the front desk directed me to Mary Miller's room at the far end of the nursing home. I wondered if I'd be allowed to take children with me, but the receptionist smiled at them and didn't say they couldn't come too.

As we moved down the long hallway we saw only elderly people—sitting in their chairs, lying on their beds, or wandering up and down the corridor. Some of the patients brightened when they saw the little boys and smiled or spoke to them. Georgie held up his bouquet for everyone to admire as he passed.

"For Mamma," he said to anyone who cared to listen.

We found Aunt Mary Miller sitting in her chair watching a TV game show. She gladly turned it off to greet Georgie. He seemed a little dazed.

"What lovely flowers, Georgie," she said, admiring them as he held them.

"For you," he said with sudden inspiration. He dropped the handful of flowers in her lap.

Aunt Mary had to wipe her tears away before she reached for her glass of drinking water.

"Will you put them in water for me, Georgie?" she asked.

Georgie placed them all in the drinking glass while his Aunt Mary looked on lovingly. When she turned her attention to Chuckie, I explained who we were and why we had come.

"Would you like to try on the robe?" I asked.

"I'll have to wait until a nurse has time to help me," she apologized with a resigned sigh. "But I do like it very much."

"Here, let me help you. We can get you into it right now."

Painfully Aunt Mary eased her arthritis-stiffened arms into the robe.

"It's pretty on you," I said. "You're all dressed up for dinner now."

"Well, it would look prettier on a young girl like you," she replied, "but we senior citizens like to dress up too, you know."

"I hope you'll have an especially good meal tonight since you dressed for dinner," I said as we left.

"Thank you so much for coming, dear," she murmured with a note of wistfulness in her voice. "I wish you could stay longer, but I know you have to get the children home before they get too hungry. Come again, won't you?"

"I'll try," I agreed. "Wave bye-bye to Aunt Mary, Georgie."

Still in his cooperative mood, Georgie waved and then made Chuckie's hand wave too. Any other time

Georgie could be in a terrible mood and I would forgive him, because at this moment he had brought a touch of sunshine to a nice old lady.

Even after the long walk down the hallway back to John, I enjoyed an afterglow. Seldom had I felt so appreciated, and it had taken such a little bit of effort on my part.

John didn't seem to pay much attention to us as we approached him. His eyes were fixed on a nearby office off the lobby. He was straining to hear some conversation.

As we came closer he held up a hand and motioned for us to keep quiet. I was puzzled, but I stopped where I stood. The words were drifting out of the office.

"We're sorry to lose you, José, because you've been a very good worker. Your new position should offer you chances for advancement, but you will be hard to replace here. Good luck."

"Did you hear?" John whispered. "What was that I said about having to be there when someone else leaves a job?"

"Why don't you try?" I urged.

GEORGIE PLAYED WALK-AROUND-THE-COFFEE-TABLE forty or fifty times while I sat nervously waiting for John to come out of the office. I could hear voices, but I couldn't understand anything they were saying.

When John finally did appear in the doorway he was shaking hands with a woman in a nurse's uniform.

"We'll see you at nine in the morning, then," she said with a smile.

"I'll be here," John agreed. "Thank you very much."

I gathered up Chuckie's teddy bear and sweater and motioned for Georgie to join us quietly.

"Did you hear that?" John asked as we left the lobby. "Just like that, I have a job."

"That's how you said it happens," I pointed out.

"But . . . if I hadn't known you, and you hadn't known Georgie, and you hadn't offered to bring the robe to Mary Miller—"

"And if you hadn't been a very qualified applicant, don't forget."

He grinned in an embarrassed way.

"I'm really glad for you, John. And I'm happy for Hill Haven too, because you'll be so good around here."

"Right," he agreed. "I can oil their stroller wheels."

"Don't laugh," I said. "I heard a squeaky wheelchair go past me."

By then we were passing the empty lot and Georgie spotted the flowers again.

"Flowers for Mamma," he shouted with joy as he darted into the dry grass.

John smiled and waited patiently while Georgie tore off a straggly little bouquet. To our surprise he carried it over to Chuckie and put it in his hands.

"For *your* mamma," he said. Then he darted back into the grass to gather more.

"For my mamma," he announced with triumph as he picked his last flower and came back to join us.

"So this is how you earn your sewing class," John commented as we walked along.

"It's not all so bad," I said. "The night out is worth it."

"It's not all so bad because you make it that way," he observed.

Autumn

SEVERAL BUSY WEEKS PASSED AND I COULD FEEL MY-self loosening up. The sewing was relaxing and fun, and I was learning enough to be able to continue at home when the course ended. But more important, at my night class I discovered a world beyond high school where raising families was a normal way of life.

I could see changes coming over John too. He was happy with his job and feeling good about his approaching graduation. It seemed as if the sadness that earlier had been so much a part of him had passed.

And then one evening John walked into my apartment and slumped into a chair. He didn't speak at all while I gathered up Chuckie's things. Feeling uncertain, I zipped Chuckie into his blanket sleeper and held him in my arms. John took the bag and we delivered Chuckie in uneasy silence to Mrs. Klopman.

As we reached the sidewalk I automatically turned

toward the school. John took my arm and said, "Not that way. We're riding."

I hadn't even noticed the car parked at the curb.

"John, you bought a car?"

He shook his head.

"You borrowed a car?"

Again he shook his head.

"You stole a car," I said, joking.

No smile.

"It's a long story," he said, opening the car door for me.

We rode without conversation.

"It *is* a nice car," I commented as we approached the school parking lot.

John pulled into a parking space.

"Sandy," he said suddenly, "I can't face a history class tonight. I feel too mixed up. How about my leaving you off for your class and I'll come back for you at nine forty-five?"

"Oh, I can get home all right," I said as I got out of the car. "If you're going home now, I wouldn't want you to have to come back for me."

"I'm not going home. I'm just going to drive around and try to make some sense in my head."

"Well . . . if you really think you'll still be out . . ."

"I may be out all night. . . . Who knows?"

Startled by this answer, I looked into John's troubled eyes. Class seemed unimportant at that moment.

"Could I come along with you? Maybe I could help."

"I don't want to talk, Sandy."

"I can keep quiet."

"Okay," he said, reaching over to open the car door.

I kept my promise. I didn't say a word. I had no idea where we were headed. The only thing I was sure of was that John needed someone, even if it was someone to be with him without talking.

John kept his eyes on the road. He seemed to know where he was going even if I didn't. He took the highway toward the coast and then turned off onto a side road. Small cottages were scattered along the way. Finally he parked at the end of the road where a path between two cabins led toward the beach.

"This stretch of beach is pretty safe," he said. "People live here all year around. I know this area."

He got out of the car.

"I'm going down to the water. Want to come?"

I nodded, still keeping my promise.

JOHN STARTED DOWN THE TRAIL. I FOLLOWED ALONG behind him. A few parts of the path were lighted by patio lamps of the cottages. Some stretches were very dark. But John moved down the trail as if he had been the one who put it there.

"That's where they lived," John said as we passed the last house before the beach.

"Who?" I asked.

John didn't answer. He just kept walking.

"I spent a lot of summers with them."

"You lived here sometimes?" I asked.

No answer.

We walked to the water's edge in silence. There he led the way to a fallen tree trunk and sat down facing the ocean. It was a rocky area and he scooped up a handful of pebbles and studied them intently. One by one, he tossed them into the water.

I sat on the other end of the tree trunk wondering how I could share his private agony. The only sounds were the splash of the pebbles as they hit the water, and the rhythmic washing of the waves. If any place could heal wounds, it seemed as if this peaceful stretch of beach could.

Every now and then John interrupted his pebble-throwing to wipe his cheek. Finally he got up and walked away from me. In the dusk I could see his silhouette . . . walking to a distant spot . . . sitting on the sand . . . his arms on his raised knees . . . his head down on his arms. I could see his body shaking with sobs. No sounds reached me. After a while he stretched out on the sand and lay very still, his face toward the sky. He didn't move.

A few stars were out and I looked up at them in wonder. For years I hadn't had a moment alone with such beauty. I was a little girl again, wishing upon the evening star.

Unexpectedly, Chuckie was in my mind. I have only one time around in life to share things like this with my child, I thought—to let him know stillness, to help him hear his own thoughts.

I was lost in dreams of my young son's childhood when I saw John slowly coming toward me. His walk was different. The tenseness was gone; his figure was almost limp.

Dropping down beside me, he said nothing.

"Are you making sense in your head?" I asked, breaking my promise not to talk.

"I'm trying."

I waited to see if he wanted to say more. For a long time it looked as if that had ended it. Then it all began to pour out.

"My parents died when I was young. . . . An aunt . . . very frail health . . . tried to raise me . . . but the Strombergs. . . . My real family was the Strombergs."

"Are they the ones who lived in that house?"

"Yes. Paul . . . their son . . . he and I were like brothers. I spent more time with them than with my aunt. She was in and out of hospitals. . . . She finally died last year."

I remembered the remark the girls had dropped in the drugstore conversation—something about his best friend being killed while he was in the service.

"Tell me about Paul," I urged.

"We understood each other. We could talk about things—anything . . . people . . . cars . . . God . . . girls . . ."

"And what happened to Paul?" I asked gently.

"We were in the service together . . . same outfit . . . both assigned as drivers at the base. We were good with engines because we had spent years rebuilding a couple of cars. Well, one day I got orders to drive an officer to a nearby post. But at the last minute they switched assignments and sent me on another job, giving those orders to Paul. A truck rammed into them and Paul died."

John stopped talking. The silence was long and painful.

"It might. . . . Why was I spared? . . . It might have been me. I want to know . . . who or what decided it should be Paul . . . who would die."

John buried his head in his hands. The rest of the story came out haltingly.

"That car we drove out here in. . . . It was Paul's. He and I rebuilt it together. Today . . . I can't believe it . . . today his parents gave it to me as a present, complete with a year's insurance."

"They must be wonderful people."

"They are."

"How does it work when you go to see them now?"

"I can hardly stand it—seeing them so heartbroken. But they say I'm their only son now and they want me to have the car."

"Maybe one reason you were spared was so you could help them recover from their loss," I suggested.

"Maybe," he answered after a long, long time. "But I don't even know how to help myself."

"Time helps," I said. After a long pause I added, "I know!"

John looked straight at me for the first time that evening.

"You do, don't you, Sandy," he said, newly aware that I was there. "I shouldn't have burdened you with my problems."

"I think people are supposed to share burdens."

"I don't know about that one, Sandy. Paul and I shared things and look at what it's like now that he's gone."

"After a while, when it begins to hurt less, you'll be able to think about all the things you had instead of what you've lost," I said, wondering if that idea could help right then.

"It's true," John said dreamily, "we did have a whole childhood together. This stretch of beach saw us through so many stages . . . so many dumb tricks . . . and a few smart ones. . . . It was our place to hide from the world, to test out the world . . . to think things out, talk things out, try things out."

John looked up but he didn't seem to be looking at me. His gaze was fixed on the wide expanse of beach.

"The next thing Paul and I were going to do was build a dune buggy . . ." His voice trailed off.

"Now they've rented the beach house and moved into a little place in town. It's as if the whole chapter is closed."

As he said this, John stood up and offered his hand to help me up. It was as if he had just closed a book.

"You should have gone to your sewing class. This evening hasn't been any good for you, Sandy."

"Let me decide that," I said as we started up the path to the car.

"TELL ME ABOUT REBUILDING THIS CAR," I SUGGESTED as we drove back to town.

"It was in terrible shape when we got it. The owner was a fool. He had managed to ruin just about everything in it. So we bought it for almost nothing and then poured hours of time into it. Since neither of us had any money we scrounged and bargained for everything we needed."

"You can almost feel its soul," I said.

"It's spooky," he added. "I can feel more than its soul. I can almost feel Paul riding in it with me."

John kept his eyes on the road and said nothing more.

After a while I broke the silence. "And now would you care to know what this evening did for me and Chuckie?"

John gave me a startled glance.

"How did Chuckie get into this evening?"

"Well, as I sat there alone on that quiet beach, Chuckie's childhood became important to me. I began worrying—what if I weren't here to teach him how to notice things? Maybe nobody else would be interested enough in his young mind to point out stars and things to him, and take him to places where he can see and feel and become a part of nature. Other people might just see to it that he learned to read and write and say please and thank you."

John shook his head the way he always did when he didn't know how to answer. We drove the rest of the way home without talking.

"Has Chuckie ever been to the beach?" John asked as we pulled up in front of Mrs. Klopman's.

"He's never been anywhere you can't get with a stroller," I said, "and that's not much farther than the shopping center or Hill Haven."

"Do you think we ought to take him to the beach next Sunday?" John asked.

That took me by surprise.

"I thought you weren't even listening. I was kind of talking to myself about Chuckie."

"I was listening, Sandy. I think we'd better take him."

I nodded in uncertain agreement.

Coming home from adult school on Wednesday I expressed my doubts to John about taking Chuckie out on Sunday.

"You don't really want to hassle around with all the bother of going somewhere with a baby, do you?"

"Why? How can it be such a hassle? He's not even a year old yet."

"That's why it is. He'll get tired and need a nap, or he'll get hungry and need a meal, or he'll cry and need holding."

"So? What's so complicated about those things? Pack him some food to eat, take a blanket for him to sleep on, and you come along to hold him if he needs comforting. Why are you making it such a big deal, Sandy?"

"I guess I just can't believe that a man would want to spend time with my baby when the baby's own father didn't even want him born in the first place."

"Sandy, you can't let one man color your whole view of men."

"It's hard not to."

By then we were home, transferring Chuckie from Mrs. Klopman's house to his own crib.

"Quit worrying about Sunday and let's have a nice day," John advised as he left. "It's not as if you were taking him along on a date, after all."

With that John was gone.

He's right, I thought. I do view things from a weird angle sometimes. Anyway, I guess John wouldn't have suggested it if he hadn't been willing to do it.

A while later I realized what he had really said—it's not a date. That's what I had to get used to. I was seventeen, but this wasn't the boy-girl bit. This was just people being together . . . mixed ages—twenty, seventeen, and nearly one.

BY THINKING ABOUT SUNDAY I GOT THROUGH THE week, overloaded with school, baby-sitting, homework, night school, laundry, and housework. When Saturday night arrived I was exhausted.

Some people are getting ready to go to parties or movies tonight, I thought to myself. And here I'll be lucky if I can make it through Chuckie's bath and diapers before I fall asleep.

As I held my slippery baby and let him splash in his bath, the thoughts that had come to me on the beach returned to haunt me.

Sandy, what have you done this week to let this little boy of yours sense the beauty of the world and the joy of living? Not a blessed thing, I had to answer. At this rate he'll be an adult before I ever have time to do anything important with him. And then what will he know about living? He'll know how to hold a spoon, and brush his teeth, and button his shirt. But will he ever have smelled a rosebud, or watched a robin eating berries, or wiggled his toes in warm sand, or run from the foaming tide, or sat quietly with people who liked him?

You'd better take time out from the rat race, I told myself. Right now. Before you forget what it's like to be human with your baby.

It sounded easy enough until Sunday morning when I started to plan for the day at the beach. At that moment I realized I didn't even know how to do such things with a baby.

I tried to think what we would need for the day. My mind drew a blank. I couldn't even make myself work out a simple list. I began to tremble. I must be getting sick, I thought. Maybe it's the flu or something. I'd better not try to go.

Chuckie started to whimper and I picked him up and held him on my lap. But my trembling didn't stop. We were huddled in the rocking chair when I heard John's knock at the door. I just sat there.

After a long time and several more knocks I heard

the doorknob turn and the door open. John slowly walked into the apartment and stood at the bedroom door.

"Ready?" he asked.

"I'm shaking all over."

"Do you feel sick?"

"I don't know. I just can't seem to think, and I keep shaking."

"Have you a thermometer around here?"

"In the medicine chest above the washbasin."

I could hear him opening the metal door and running the water.

"Here, put this in your mouth and don't talk till it's out."

Silently John went around tidying things up. Then he returned to take the thermometer.

"You don't have a fever," he announced. He studied me closely. "What's the matter?"

I shook my head. The trembling had stopped while I watched John move around the room.

"I don't know. I just started to crumble like a cookie this morning when I tried to think what I should pack for us. I couldn't even make a simple list. All I could do was shake."

"Sandy," he said as he put his arm around my shoulders, "you have too much responsibility too young. . . . I think that's what's getting you down."

"So, what shall I do? Tell Chuckie to take care of himself today—Mamma needs a day off?"

"Well, we can get a little bit of a day off for you, at least, if we get you out of here."

John stood beside me patting my shoulder. I wasn't sure whether he was feeling fatherly or more like a coach saying "Come on, team, let's get in there and give it the old try." After a moment he squatted down by the chair and spoke directly to me, his hand stroking Chuckie's hair and his eyes meeting mine.

"You do *want* to go out for the day, don't you, Sandy? I'm not trying to make you do something you don't want to do?"

"I want to."

"Then let's get a few things together and go. It's just not all that huge an undertaking."

Again he went into action.

"Chuckie will need a blanket to lie on and one to put over him when he takes a nap," he said as he laid two folded blankets on the bed. "And a sweater. And his snowsuit, maybe. It's not a warm day.

"How many diapers will he need?" he asked as he counted his way down the pile of folded laundry.

"You'll need a jacket or sweater for yourself and sunglasses maybe. Why don't you get your things and meet me in the kitchen?"

I set Chuckie down and did as I was told.

"Now, for Chuckie what do you want? Some milk? A bottle of water, a few jars of baby food, and some cookies or toast or something. You pick his food and I'll take care of us."

As I put the baby food and bottles into Chuckie's insulated bag John got a paper sack and started filling it. He nosed his way around the kitchen discovering some fruit, cookies, bread, lunch meat, and sodas.

"Let's go," he said.

"You mean we're ready just like that?"

"Just like that. Nothing to panic about, is it?"

"It looked so hopeless an hour ago."

"Well, if you're going to care for a baby, you're going to have to find easy ways to do things, Sandy. Figure out what is important and don't worry about all the other things."

"Thank you for your prescription, doctor," I said.

"Fill that prescription right now and start taking it," he answered in a professional tone.

It was a third John Nolan speaking. Not the sad one, and not the friendly one. This John Nolan was taking charge—serious and responsible.

"And wait till you see my fees," he added, glancing over at me with a new kind of grin.

There was nothing left to do but laugh. Together we laughed until Chuckie joined in too. And that was when I was sure that Dr. Nolan prescribed very good medicine.

"DO YOU WANT TO GO TO THE SAME BEACH WE WENT to before?" John asked as we approached the turnoff in the highway.

"I don't see how there could be a nicer spot," I said.

"We'll have to carry Chuckie and the food. Okay?"

"I think it will be worth it when we get there," I answered.

We parked at the end of the road and laid out the things to be carried.

"I'll take Chuckie if he'll let me," John suggested.

"I'm afraid he's shy," I said doubtfully, "but let's try."

I started to hand him over to John. Instantly Chuckie clung to my neck and began to cry.

John looked hurt as he bent to pick up the bags instead.

"Children take time on those things, you know," I hurried to explain. "And, of course, this little boy doesn't know much about men."

John didn't answer. He turned and led the way down the trail to the beach. I saw him studying the Stromberg cottage as we passed it.

We followed him over to a sheltered area surrounded on three sides by sand dunes. The other side was open to the ocean view. John stooped to spread a blanket for us.

Chuckie, finding the beach new and strange, was in no hurry to move away from my lap. In fact, he clung to me fiercely when he sensed John's steady gaze upon him. But John wasn't interested in trying to win him over.

John shifted his eyes to me instead. I could feel him staring at me, and I was becoming uncomfortable. I didn't know him well enough to know what it meant.

Finally John broke the silence.

"Maybe it's good that way," he said thoughtfully. "Maybe . . ."

"What's good?" I asked.

"What you said about Chuckie."

I searched back in my mind trying to remember what had been said about Chuckie. We hadn't even spoken all the way down the trail, and at that point my mind had been retracing the steps John and I had taken in the dark just a few nights earlier.

"I don't think I know what you mean," I said, feeling apologetic.

"You said this little boy doesn't know much about men."

This harmless remark of John's instantly started something that neither of us had expected. Ever since Chuckie's birth there had been moments when suddenly I felt touchy and quarrelsome. I would twist people's words and make them come out sounding like insults aimed at me.

"So what are you telling me?"

I knew I was on a collision course, but I was unable to change it. Maybe at that moment I didn't want to.

"I'm just saying," John continued in his patient way, "that since Chuckie doesn't have a father I'm glad he doesn't have a string of his mother's boyfriends passing through his life."

"Do you think you know everything I do?" I asked hotly. "Everyone I see?"

I was stupidly contradicting what I had said just a few seconds earlier. I felt like a volcano, full of pressure and ready to blow its top.

"Oh, quit playing games, Sandy," John answered in disgust.

"Besides," I continued with my irrational line of thinking, "what would it be to *you* if there were men in my life?"

My flare-up had started quickly. There had been nothing to cause it except my own tangled emotions. Now it was rapidly dying in my hands.

"You don't own me," I announced, trying in vain to keep my fading fury alive. But the real hurt was rising to the surface to replace the anger. "I'm not even your girl friend. . . . You've said so. . . . I belong to myself . . . to Chuckie . . . and we get along just fine alone."

"Yeah. Like you were this morning when I arrived!"

Chuckie, quick to sense the tension around him, began to cry. This turned our sand dune into total bedlam. I held him close, but there was little comfort in my rocking. I wanted to scream too.

John stood up and strode away across the sand. In seconds he was gone. Out of sight. Chuckie and I were left with a lonely sand dune, a deserted stretch of beach, miles of churning surf . . . and my own miserable moodiness.

A LONG HOUR PASSED. CHUCKIE QUIETED DOWN AND SO did I. I rocked him gently and he started one of his soft humming songs. It was hard to believe we were the same two who were in such turmoil a short while earlier. His gentle little song made the beach serene again. Soon he was asleep.

I looked around me. The rolling curve of the sand dunes formed a graceful pattern against the overcast sky. Patches of wild grass moved softly in the wind. Purple flowers on the verbena plants contrasted with the soft tones of the sand. And it was quiet.

Eventually I saw John coming slowly up the beach. What, I wondered, do you say after a scene like that? Compared to the man walking toward me, I was a mixed-up child. There was no excuse for my stupid explosion—no way to justify it.

"Is he all right?" John asked, looking at the sleeping child on the blanket.

"He's fine," I assured him.

John sat down beside me, closer than he had ever sat before. He handed me a small bouquet of wild flowers he had picked.

"I've done lots of things on this beach," John said, "but I never thought I'd find myself here fighting with a mother and child."

I lifted the bouquet to my face to smell the fragrance.

"Why did we get into that idiot fight?" he asked in a soft voice.

"It's my fault. I'm touchy and hard to get along with sometimes. And I don't want to be."

"You're living so tense, Sandy. You're going to have to learn to calm down. You're too young to be a bundle of nerves."

I nodded.

"Here, I'll show you some good medicine," John said. "Leave Chuckie sleeping there and move back a few feet so you can lean against the sand dune."

He spread the extra blanket out and motioned for me to move to it. The angle of the dune was exactly right so that I could see the ocean, the sky, and the sand—nothing else, except an occasional gull circling over the water. John stretched out comfortably with his hands under his head like a pillow.

"How's that?" he asked. "This spot has seen me through a lot of problems. I used to come here all the time to think—to sort things out in my head."

"I've needed a place like this for a long time," I admitted. "Ever since I got married, in fact. From that point on my life has been a mess."

"I can see how it was a mess for a while," John agreed, "but what's such a mess about it now?"

"I feel like some sort of freak—a mother at seventeen, while the other girls are having fun."

"You're only a freak if you think you are. And the other girls aren't having that much fun," John said. "I'll bet they think they have problems too."

"Maybe."

"But you *are* going to have to get out more, Sandy. You and Chuckie both need that. We could do this on some other Sundays if you want to."

I smiled at his suggestion, but I couldn't believe it would work out.

"What's worrying you, Sandy?" he asked after a few moments of silence.

"Do you really want to know?"

"Yes."

"Well," I started with some doubt in my voice, "with a baby and all those responsibilities I'm not someone that a man would want as a date or as a girl friend."

John looked over at me with a strange expression.

"How . . . just tell me, how would *you* like to be at a party and have to leave at ten o'clock because your date's baby-sitting arrangements had run out or something?"

John looked baffled.

"So, you see," I said as if it were the final word on the subject, "that rules me out as any kind of fun. But you . . . you're a young, very eligible male and sooner or later you're going to want an attractive girl friend. And you shouldn't be stuck, then, with a mother and child that you feel you have to be kind to."

"You really do think crazy, Sandy," John said, shaking his head. "Now you're talking us out of a friendship on the grounds that someday I might want to marry someone and you'd be in the way."

"Well?" I asked, but John interrupted.

"The problem is you think too much, Sandy, and a lot of it's wrong."

I sat up straight, all ready to head into battle again.

"Come on back here and calm down," John said, pulling me down by the shoulders. His arm was behind me as I landed. He kept it around my shoulders.

"Now, start changing your thinking about men," he ordered.

I wasn't sure what he was leading up to.

"Relax," he said. "See how it feels to lie here and look at the sand and the sky and the sea with another human being close by who cares about you."

"This is something I'll have to learn," I said softly. "It's different from what I've had before."

Comfortably I settled down on the sand dune close to John. He was right. It was good medicine. Then, just as I was beginning to breathe easily, Chuckie stirred.

He opened his eyes, looked with surprise at his surroundings, stretched a bit, and began to cry. Immediately I was tense again, knowing he would have to be fed. He was late for his lunch. Quickly I sat upright.

"Relax, Sandy."

"I can't. He needs lunch."

"So . . . relax. Is lunch such a big deal?"

"It is if you're ten months old and hungry!"

"Bring him back here and let him relax too. He may like a nice easygoing lunch for a change."

I moved Chuckie back to the other blanket and opened a couple of jars of baby food. John propped him up against the sand dune so I could spoon-feed him. Chuckie seemed to love it all. He ate more than he ever wanted at home. Then I gave him his bottle and he held it for himself, making cheerful noises as he emptied it.

"There's a happy man," John said as Chuckie dropped his empty bottle with a final flourish. "See, it's no big deal. Have fun."

We did. All three of us.

The afternoon flew. Chuckie crawled around in the sand, digging little finger holes. He sat down in front of us and laughed while John buried his tiny feet in the sand. John's good-natured kidding kept both Chuckie and me smiling.

"I hate for it to end, Sandy, but we'd better be starting home," John finally announced. "At this season the late afternoon wind is bad here."

We packed our belongings and trudged up the path to the car.

"You know, Chuckie will be much easier to take places when he can walk instead of having to be carried," John said as we reached the road. "There are some fun places we can take him when he's a little older."

I grinned as I listened to this pleasant man making plans to take my young son somewhere in the future.

JOHN GLANCED AT HIS GAS GAUGE AS WE PASSED A STATION near my home.

"Oops, it's empty," he said as he stopped the car and backed up to the pumps. "You don't mind waiting a few minutes even though we're so close to home, do you, Sandy?"

"Of course not."

I took Chuckie and his diaper bag and went into the station rest room. I could hear the gas pump ringing off the gallons. I heard another car pull in and a second pump started.

"John!" a girl's voice called as a car door slammed.

"Linda," John's surprised voice answered, "I thought you had a job in another city."

Apparently they were moving away from the rest-room window. The conversation became faint and I couldn't catch any of it.

I stood there in panic, clutching Chuckie and wondering what to do next. Sooner or later John and Linda were bound to meet again somewhere, but why did it have to be with me along? And why did it have to be at the end of such a perfect afternoon?

Maybe she'll reclaim him, I thought to myself. If she caught him once, she probably could again. I'm told she manages to have her own way with most people, especially men.

There were few choices left to me. I couldn't huddle in the rest room forever. Finally, making a quick decision, I opened the rest-room door and stepped out, carrying Chuckie and his bag. John and Linda were talking on the other side of her car.

Hurrying through the station, I turned back toward them and called, "It was nice to bump into you again, John." Then I turned and walked down the sidewalk toward home . . . very casually, I hoped.

My heart was pounding and I felt sick inside.

He loved her enough to be engaged to her once, I said to myself. She's a beautiful girl, after all. That hasn't changed.

I hadn't walked far before John's car pulled up beside me. He leaned over, opened the door, and helped pull Chuckie into the car.

"What on earth did you do that for, Sandy?"

"I didn't want to embarrass you."

"Why would you embarrass me?"

"I didn't think you wanted it to look to Linda as if you were taking out some girl with a baby. She might even have decided it was your baby. I didn't want you to have to explain a lot of things to her."

John had a look of disbelief on his face.

"And besides, I thought maybe you had things to talk about—old times or bad times or something. I didn't want to butt in."

"You really do believe you're poison to be with, don't you, Sandy?"

"I don't think men want to explain a girl and a baby to former fiancées."

"I would have been proud to introduce you to Linda and tell her that we had taken Chuckie to play in the sand dunes. Linda could think anything she liked. I couldn't care less. I owe her no explanations."

"She *is* very beautiful," I said, still unsure of John's feelings toward Linda.

"She is," he agreed, "if you like that kind of beauty. I found it dazzling at one time."

That seemed to be the end of Linda. John reached over and tousled Chuckie's hair.

"You learned about beaches today, didn't you, old boy?"

Chuckie, who had started the day by crying when John offered to carry him, sealed the afternoon with a broad smile.

John grinned back at him as he pulled up in front of my apartment.

"Good-by, you two," he said as I closed the car door and thanked him.

Winter

THE END OF THE NIGHT SCHOOL QUARTER WAS FAST approaching and the pressure was building up in John. His final exams were worrying him because his graduation depended upon them. And his job at Hill Haven left him too little study time.

Although he took me to classes regularly, he was changing. Our night school evenings were a time to be together . . . but actually we weren't together at all. We were in our own little bubbles, close but isolated.

There had been no time for the beach. No time for talking after classes. Even Chuckie's first birthday passed unnoticed except for the little party Mom and I had with him. My greatest hope was that graduation would bring John some relief from pressure and then maybe we could take up where we had left off.

"Graduation ceremonies are going to be on the first Friday in December," John told me casually as I got out of the car one evening. "I'd be glad if you'd come."

"Of course I'll come," I said, indignant that he should even wonder if I would.

Immediately I started preparations for the big night. Since John had no family to celebrate with him, Chuckie and I would give him a party. It would be a surprise.

I scrimped and saved to set aside some money to buy the party food. And then when I saw a beautiful book of color photographs of the world's finest beaches, I used all the food money I had saved to buy the book as a graduation gift for John.

Every time I opened my dresser drawer the handsomely wrapped gift book made me feel warm and excited. Graduation night would be a time to remember.

As the evening drew nearer I planned how I would spend the second round of food money I had managed to save. The best idea seemed to be a late supper. Chuckie wouldn't be able to stay up for it, of course, but he could have his time with John earlier.

The day before graduation I shopped for the food, set the table with my wedding gifts, fixed the refrigerator foods, and arranged blue candles to match the flowers I picked in the apartment house garden.

Finally, with enormous satisfaction, I put the last stitch in Chuckie's new outfit and gave it a pressing.

This evening was to be a perfect climax to John's long struggle for his diploma. Not everyone would care for a little home party on such an occasion . . . but a man who enjoyed quiet beaches probably would like it.

As the graduates assembled on the stage, Chuckie sat quietly on my lap. I was afraid he might be restless or noisy, but instead he felt shy in the large crowd. He sucked his thumb through the long speeches, and only began to come alive as the audience applauded each graduate.

It was an exciting moment when John's name was called and he stepped forward to recive his diploma. My eyes got misty and my throat choked up. I clapped timidly, feeling certain that Chuckie and I were John's only rooting section. But as he left the center of the stage to return to his seat, a round of applause came from the other side of the auditorium. John looked over in surprise.

The ceremonies came to a close and the audience gathered in the lobby to wait for the graduates to join them. Nervously I held Chuckie and watched the doors that John might come through. He didn't know anything about my party plans for him. I was going to surprise him when he took me home. He would, I was sure, since he had asked me to come to the graduation.

When I spotted him coming toward us down the long corridor, he looked tall and proud. This graduation mattered a great deal to him. Chuckie and I started to press forward to meet him. At the same time a group of seven or eight other people broke through the crowd and rushed toward him.

Dumbfounded, I watched it all happen. The crowd was led by Linda—a bubbly, laughing Linda.

"Johnny, congratulations," she shouted gaily as she

threw her arms around him. "Look, the old gang all came to see you through it. And now we're taking you with us to celebrate. We have it all planned. More of the old crowd is meeting us for a party at my place. It took you longer than the rest of us, so that's why we have to celebrate extra hard tonight."

John hadn't said a word. How could he!

"So come on, everybody," she gushed, "let's give Johnny a real old-time graduation night. Off to my place."

Linda motioned for the group to follow her to the exit.

John didn't move.

"Johnny, come on. Hurry up. They're all leaving."

She held his arm close to her and gave him a pouty little expression. John was looking over the crowd in the lobby.

I managed to catch his eye. He turned to Linda and said something. Reluctantly she let go and John came toward Chuckie and me.

"You came," he said to me. "Thanks."

"Apparently so did a lot of other friends," I said, hoping my bitterness wasn't too obvious.

"I can't even remember the names of most of them," John said, looking at the floor.

"Well, the tall one is Linda," I said with careful sarcasm. "Surely you remember her?"

"Don't sound like that, Sandy," he ordered. "Please don't?" he asked, trying to soften his tone. "I didn't know she was coming or planning a party or anything. I just took her for a ride last week because she said she wanted to explain a few things she hadn't put in her last letter to me. She inquired at that time when graduation would be. That's all."

"Yeah, well, have a ball," I said as I put Chuckie's coat around him and started for the door.

"We'll drop you and Chuckie off on our way," John suggested as if it were a weak afterthought.

"Please don't!"

I turned quickly, pulled Chuckie's collar up around his neck, and headed out into the cold night for the miserable walk home.

FORTUNATELY THE LONG WALK GAVE ME TIME TO WORK off some of my fury and some of the hurt before I actually had to open the door and face my dead graduation party. I made plans as I walked.

First I would scoop everything off the table and dump it in the garbage. Then I would set fire to the book about beaches and watch it burn.

As I shifted Chuckie's weight from one side to the other my anger cooled down. Exhaustion took its place instead. By the time I reached my apartment I could only sink into a chair and stare at the unlit candles.

Earlier I had felt like screaming at the whole world. Now I just put Chuckie to bed in his crib and lay down on my own bed, staring at the ceiling. I might have felt better if I could cry, cry, cry. But the hurt went too deep for that. I was beyond crying; I was numb.

It was a long night of fitful sleep. I kept waking up, feeling miserable, and dropping off again. Finally a few rays of sunshine began filtering through the eastern window and there was another day to be lived . . . or endured.

The party table was there to mock me. And my wedding gifts. Beautiful and useless. Time to pack them up again. Maybe we'd have a party when Chuckie turned eighteen or something.

As I folded the cloth and put the silverware in the case I could see Linda's face laughing at me. I could even hear her saying, "Johnny, what did you ever see in that girl with the baby? All she could ever do is tie you down and keep you from having any more fun. Fun, Johnny. That's what we'll have now. Fun. We lost too much time while you were in the service. Now we'll make up for it."

Clearly I could hear Linda urging John on to the carefree life. But for some reason I could never hear John's replies. All I could ever catch of John in these imaginary scenes was the look in his eyes as he spoke to me in the lobby while the party crowd was waiting for him to join them. The look was deep and wistful, like some animal, trapped and unable to understand what was holding it.

"Well, Chuckie," I said as my young man opened his sleepy eyes and smiled at the new day. "We're back to going it alone again. We've been along this route before. I guess we know the way."

Chuckie climbed to his feet and rattled the side of

the crib. I went over to him with some dry clothes to start his morning. He was full of wiggles and bounces.

"But it seems more lonely than it was before, somehow."

Then the truth dawned on me. It was all over. Everything. It wasn't just that I had lost John. My night school class was over . . . no more times with the friendly older women . . . no more evenings out . . . none of the things that had made me feel alive during the past few months. Just like a book. When you've read the last page there's nothing left to do but close the book and put it down. At that point it never occurred to me that there are other books you can pick up and start.

TIME, WHICH HAD BEEN MOVING TOO FAST AS NIGHT school approached the end, now started moving at a slow crawl. The days at school seemed to last forever. The evenings at home alone with Chuckie and my homework and my housework were even longer.

Christmas was only days away. I knew I should try to make it a season of warmth and happiness for Chuckie. As I looked at his life, filled with nobody much except a mother and a grandmother, I knew I needed to find some way to help him catch the spirit of giving.

There had been a little of this in his friendship with Georgie. They were learning to share toys and share fun. We'll have to do more with Georgie, I decided.

One day I stopped to chat with Mrs. Klopman as she pulled into her driveway.

"I've just been over visiting with Aunt Mary at Hill Haven," she said. "She asked about you and Chuckie. I guess you made quite an impression on her and several other patients. They're still talking about your pleasant smile and the happy faces of the two boys."

"She did seem to appreciate a little attention," I agreed, remembering the warm glow I had felt after our short visit with Aunt Mary. "I'll try to get over to see her again."

I had made the offer before I realized that there was more to it than seeing Aunt Mary. A visit to Hill Haven meant I might also run into John. I didn't know what his working hours were since he had finished night school.

At first I was chilled by the prospect of seeing John again. I had caught occasional glimpses of him passing by with Linda in his car. But we never met.

I kept the thought of visiting Aunt Mary in the back of my mind for a while, hoping it would go away or something. It wasn't until it dawned upon me that Linda was dominating my life, too, that I made my big decision.

Even if John's and my paths did have to cross at Hill Haven, why not? Linda was no reason to cut Aunt Mary out of my life.

"WHY DON'T WE FIX SOME CHRISTMAS COOKIES FOR Aunt Mary Miller?" I suggested to Chuckie on Saturday morning. He was always for cookies. So I baked a batch and decorated them with colored candies.

"Let's walk over to Hill Haven with these, Chuckie."

He hurried to get the stroller from the closet and tried to unfold it.

As it had before, our route to Hill Haven took us past John's place. We stayed on the opposite side of the street. As we passed it I could hear John's voice echoing in my mind . . . *I'll go up and get the oil. . . . There you are, no squeak to drive you crazy now. . . . I've been job-hunting all day. . . . Could I walk along with you?*

When finally I did dare to look up to his second-story window, there was no one in sight. The windows were closed. The drapes were pulled.

When we passed the vacant lot where Georgie had picked the flowers Chuckie recognized it instantly. He pointed, waved his arms, and said a word that sounded something like flower. I stopped the stroller and let him climb out. He waded through the weeds toward a patch of straggly blooms. They weren't real wild flowers. For years people had been dumping garden cuttings in the lot. They had sprouted and thrived. Now they had become wild garden flowers.

It was harder than Chuckie had anticipated to pick most of the flowers. He worked away, tugging at some, bending others. When, as a last resort, he started biting the stems, I went to his rescue. Together we picked a respectable bouquet.

I knew I would feel uneasy going to Hill Haven and taking a chance on seeing John. But I didn't realize that the feeling would become total panic as we turned up the driveway and approached the front door. I was all ready to turn and run when I heard John's voice calling me.

Looking around, I couldn't tell where it had come from.

"Over here . . . in the clump of bushes to the left of the door."

By then he had climbed through the tangled branches and stood on the driveway, holding a large pair of hedge clippers.

"How are you, Sandy?" he asked, looking down at Chuckie. Our eyes did not meet.

"Fine," I said. "We brought some cookies to Aunt Mary Miller. People in nursing homes get lonesome at Christmastime."

"I know," John answered. "I see it every day."

Hurriedly waving good-by, I opened the front door and started down the long hallway to Aunt Mary's room. I couldn't have handled any more conversation with John.

The scene inside had not changed. So many blank faces . . . shriveled bodies . . . people whose lives had come to a standstill.

We had a pleasant visit with Aunt Mary, who was one of the few who were aware of all that went on. She noticed how Chuckie had grown. She liked the way I was wearing my hair. She admired each of the flowers Chuckie had brought her and tried to teach him the names.

After our visit we had to pass through that lineup of faces again. By the time we were out the door I was haunted by what I had seen. I wasn't sure whether I would try to forget it—put it out of my mind—or whether I would feel compelled to come back and help.

BUT ONCE CHUCKIE AND I WERE OUTSIDE IN THE SUNshine, it all seemed unreal. The faces back at Hill Haven became shadowy. Reality was the little boy walking beside me pushing his own stroller until he became tired enough to want to ride.

And so I went home to join the world, putting the lonely ones out of my mind. I went about the everyday business of living, but somehow it wasn't all that great.

During that brief moment at Hill Haven I had felt lucky. I had life, health, youth, and a strong, sweet baby. Compared with the ones who had lost all those things, I was rich. But compared with the other high school seniors, I was living in chains. Slowly my own depression was creeping up on me.

Each day I became more and more blue. Nothing seemed to matter very much. School certainly didn't. Or the housework. Not even the tiny Christmas tree I bought for our apartment gave me a twinge of excitement.

I'm dead, I thought to myself with horror one day. I might just as well be sitting in one of those wheelchairs in the nursing home corridor.

That did it. At that moment my last visit to Aunt Mary came to my mind. What was it I had said to myself as I left? Forget them . . . pretend you never saw them . . . or . . . or . . . and this other possibility dawned on me slowly . . . or go back and do something to help.

My decision was sudden.

"Chuckie, we're going to decorate this Christmas tree and take it over to Hill Haven."

I fixed it up with all the little inexpensive things I could think of to make the tree colorful and festive. After I slipped a pillowcase over it to keep the wind from blowing the decorations off, we carried the tiny tree to Hill Haven.

Aunt Mary was so touched that she started to weep. Chuckie, sensing her mood, was ready to join her in a good cry, but Aunt Mary quickly distracted him by admiring each little ornament.

"This tree is beautiful, dear," she said as she wiped a tear from her cheek. "It reminds me of the little trees we used to cut in the woods when I was a girl. We decorated them for the elderly shut-ins of our church."

Aunt Mary became silent. Her eyes were misty as she moved to some time in the past and some faraway place.

"Sandy," she said as she snapped back to the present, "I can't be selfish and enjoy this tree all alone. I think I'll put it in the sun-room where all the patients can share its beauty. Do you mind if I do that?"

"Of course not. I'm glad if it will bring pleasure to a lot of people. Do you want me to take it to the sun-room now?"

"No, I want that fun myself," she answered. "Could you help me into a wheelchair? We'll take it down together."

Chuckie helped push the wheelchair down the corridor. Aunt Mary held the tree on her lap.

"Let's stop at the nurses' desk and show them what we have," Aunt Mary suggested.

"Mrs. Miller," one of the nurses said with a twinkle in her eye, "what on earth are you doing riding around with a Christmas tree on your lap?"

"Sandy brought it to me and I'm going to put it in the sun-room where everyone can enjoy it."

"How wonderful!" the nurse said to me. "You know, we have several big boxes full of Christmas decorations that a community organization gave us one year, but we are so busy with the patients that we never get the decorations put up."

She followed us into the sun-room to make a place for the tree.

"It's very kind of you," she added as she lifted the tree into place. "So many of these patients are forgotten people."

On a quick impulse I turned to the nurse. "I'd be glad to come over after school on a couple of days and put up those decorations for you," I offered.

"We'd be delighted," she said.

On Monday as I left for school I kissed Chuckie good-by and made him a promise.

"When I get home this afternoon we are going over to Hill Haven and make things pretty. Be a good boy for Grandma."

He waved and then turned to Grandma.

"Go bye-bye?"

"After your nap, Chuckie," I heard her explaining as I closed the door.

When I returned later in the day Chuckie was at the door to greet me.

"Go bye-bye. Hill Haven!"

"Yes. Right now," I assured him. "Get your snowsuit and stroller."

I set down my books and went to check on our dinner supplies. Chuckie came into the kitchen pushing his stroller and dragging his snowsuit.

"I'm so glad you're helping people, Sandy," my mother said as we left. "You've always had a way with people in trouble."

That's a laugh, I thought to myself as we walked toward Hill Haven. I don't even know how to help myself out of trouble.

To my relief, John was nowhere in sight at Hill Haven. I noticed that the landscaping around the place was looking neater and wondered if that was John's work. I noticed that there were no squeaky wheelchairs in the hallway and again I thought John's hand had been there.

Chuckie and I stood at the front desk and waited

for the nurse to look up. When she did, she couldn't conceal her surprise.

"You did come back!" she exclaimed.

"I said I would."

"A lot of people have *said* they would, but you're the first to do it."

Then she turned to the intercom on the desk.

"Sally, would you ask John if he could get the boxes of Christmas decorations out of the storage room? We have a young lady up here who is going to put them up for us.

"He'll be up with them in just a moment, I'm sure," she said to me. "Have you ever met our man John?"

"Yes," I said in a weak voice.

"Don't you want to sit down while you wait?" she asked.

"We'll go and visit with Mary Miller while we wait," I suggested.

I was sincerely hoping that John would bring up the boxes and disappear again while I was in the other room.

Aunt Mary was overjoyed to see Chuckie again. When I explained the reason for our visit she got right into the spirit of the season.

"If you can help me into a wheelchair, I'll come out and watch you decorate, dear. And maybe I can help entertain Chuckie so you won't have to watch him so closely."

"That will be a wonderful help," I said.

Already I could sense her hopes of being able to do something useful.

By the time we reached the front desk the boxes were there and John was not. I knelt over one of the large cartons on the floor and began to check its contents. There was an assortment of ornaments, so I began to plan in my mind where the different things should go.

When I turned around a moment later to see why Chuckie was so quiet, Chuckie was not in sight. One of the other boxes was open, however, and a tinsel garland was trailing out from it . . . and still moving.

I followed the tinsel with my eyes. Fifty feet down the corridor, at the end of the garland, there was Chuckie walking and tugging. By then it had reached its full length, so he dropped the tinsel and toddled back.

Aunt Mary was watching it all in fascination. My own instinct was to scold. My child—messing around and getting things out of order. But suddenly I thought how it seemed from Chuckie's point of view. We came to decorate, so he was decorating.

"Here, Chuckie," I called, trying to act reasonably, "take this one next, will you?"

He caught the idea instantly and walked away again with the second length of tinsel stretching out behind him. This became a good game. I stood at the box, untangling garlands as they came out, and Chuckie spread them down the hall ready for hanging.

Standing on a chair from the sun-room, I draped

the garlands along the corridor—to the top of each room's door frame, and dipped them gracefully in between rooms.

Chuckie let out excited squeals which brought quite a few wheelchairs to doorways. Some of the patients showed their delight. Some just stared in their blank way. And some of the ones who had returned to their childhood giggled.

"Don't they look pretty, Chuckie?" Aunt Mary said to him, pointing up at the tinsel as he toddled past her and traveled the full length of the corridor.

"Well, that's one day's work," I commented as I surveyed it all. "Let's check what's left in the other boxes."

Chuckie squatted down by one of the boxes and lifted out little things he liked.

"There seem to be enough individual ornaments here for each room to have something on its door," I said to the nurse who was standing over the boxes and me. "We'll be back tomorrow to finish the job."

We left without ever having seen John.

THE NEXT AFTERNOON CHUCKIE AND I HURRIED TO Hill Haven to finish our job. As we entered the front door we felt a festive air about the place. More people than usual were sitting in the corridors in their wheelchairs.

We walked between the patients to the end of the hall where we had stored the boxes.

"I'll get the masking tape right away," the nurse called after me.

Chuckie and I knelt on the floor and started to count the door ornaments. With Chuckie's help it even took talent to count. Sometimes he handed me two, sometimes he put things back in the box instead of in the pile, and sometimes he would take an ornament and wander off to look into a patient's room. But there was joy in his helping.

Just as I was wondering if the masking tape had been forgotten, I heard footsteps behind me. Turning around, I found myself looking up at John. He was holding a giant roll of tape.

"I didn't know it was you decorating this place," he said.

"Well, Chuckie's helping."

"They only told me to have the boxes ready because somebody was going to use them. I had no idea . . ."

I smiled at the way we were finally meeting.

"It's making a difference, Sandy. The patients feel it."

"So do Chuckie and I."

John handed me the roll of tape and I turned to the boxes. He stood there in uncomfortable silence, looking as if he wanted to say something more. I busied myself with the ornaments, not knowing how to help the situation.

Just then the stillness was shattered by several loud blasts from an automobile horn.

"What idiot would be out there blowing his horn in front of a nursing home?" the nurse said in disgust.

"I'll go see," John volunteered.

"Point out the QUIET ZONE signs posted along the sidewalk," she told him as he went out the door.

Just out of curiosity I went to a window in the sunroom to watch what was going on. The scene turned out to be unforgettable.

There was Linda, parked right beside the QUIET ZONE sign. John tore out to the curb, obviously angry. I watched as he pointed to the sign and started talking and motioning. Linda turned pouty and looked wounded. She leaned over and opened the car door, apparently telling John to come inside to do his talking. He sat down in the front seat, still making angry gestures. Linda moved over closer to him and put her arm around his shoulders. I could just hear Linda soft-talking him with her "Oh, come on, Johnny, what are you so mad about?"

And then I watched with enormous satisfaction as John lifted her arm off his shoulders, dropped it on her lap, opened the car door, and got out. Linda looked furious. John shot his last angry words at her and slammed the car door. She started her engine and gunned it. John turned and stormed away. Linda, as a final display of contempt, leaned on her horn and drove off, the sound fading into a distant wail. John disappeared into a side entrance of Hill Haven.

I DIDN'T SEE JOHN AGAIN FOR A LONG TIME. CHUCKIE and I returned after Christmas to take down the decorations and store them away for another year. We went often to see Aunt Mary. But in all those visits there was never a glimpse of John.

Finally one day I got up enough nerve to ask the nurse why.

"Doesn't John Nolan work here anymore?"

"Yes, he certainly does. He's very important to us."

"I never see him when I come," I said.

"Well, that's because he has started paramedical training at Fairview Community College. He works a split shift here—part before classes and the rest in the evening."

"Is that a long course?"

"Two years and an internship, I think, Sandy."

"Is he happy about his decision?" I asked, hoping I wouldn't sound too interested in him.

"He says it's great. Apparently he's found his way."

She was being so cooperative about answering my questions that I decided to go for the big one.

"By the way, has that girl who sat outside honking her horn been back?"

"Linda? She used to sit around on a lot of days waiting for John to finish work. But she hasn't been back since the horn-honking episode."

That was enough good news. I decided to quit while I was ahead. Chuckie and I went down to see Aunt Mary and then walked home.

We began to fall into a regular routine. Three times a week after school Chuckie and I would go over to Hill Haven. Usually Chuckie would pick some flowers in the vacant lot and take them to Aunt Mary and several other patients who were becoming his friends.

These patients fell into the routine too. Chuckie would show up with his fistful of assorted flowers. His elderly friends began keeping paper cups on their bedside tables. Chuckie would make the rounds, letting the patients choose flowers from his bouquet to fill their cups. While he tended his flower route I usually did little personal things for some of the patients with special needs.

Chuckie became a favorite topic of conversation with the few patients who gathered in their wheelchairs in the sun-room. One elderly grandfather—a man with a twinkle in his eye—especially enjoyed Chuckie. After Chuckie had passed out his supply of flowers, this gentleman would lean over to a shriveled-up little woman in the wheelchair next to his.

"What did the florist deliver to you today, Jane?"

"Two daisies and a dandelion," she answered with a vague look.

"Your admirer must be very serious then, Jane."

One afternoon in the springtime we arrived at Hill Haven later than usual. Chuckie immediately went about his flower business. I was helping a patient in the room nearest the front desk when I heard a conversation drifting through the open doorway.

"Hello, John. What brings you in so early today?"

"The instructor was sick, so they canceled our class for the day. What's new here?"

"It's not new, but our flower boy is here passing out joy."

"I've never seen it happen," John answered. "I just get word of it secondhand from the patients. He brings good medicine, doesn't he?"

"He's a delightful little boy. But when you know his mother you easily see why he is."

I couldn't hear any response to that one. But the nurse continued. "Why don't you sneak in quietly and watch how it's done, John? You'll pick up some good medical techniques."

"Okay."

I heard John's footsteps passing the door and moving toward the sun-room. Quickly I finished my job and went to sneak a peek.

I could see the action through the crack in the door without being seen myself. John sat down in a wheelchair holding a paper cup in his hands. Chuckie was moving around to the patients, lifting his bouquet for them to choose from.

The little shriveled woman got her usual two daisies and a dandelion. The friendly grandfather had some cornflowers. I held my breath as Chuckie approached John. To him John might be just another stranger. He was so young when we had been to the beach that he probably wouldn't remember that day

—and most of the other times when John had been around, Chuckie was asleep.

Chuckie stood in front of John's wheelchair and gazed intently up into John's face. Something seemed to pass between them. Silently he held up his bouquet for John to pick a flower. John reached down and started to take a pink geranium. Chuckie shook his head.

"No?" John asked. "Which one, then?"

Chuckie pointed to the one rose in his bouquet—a full-blown deep-red one.

"This one?" John asked earnestly. "Why?"

Chuckie, still too young to be much of a talker, looked steadily at John and said nothing.

"Why this one, Chuckie?" John insisted.

"It's . . . pwetty!"

Chuckie pulled the rose from his bouquet, dropping a few loose blossoms at the same time, and placed the deep-red flower in John's paper cup.

"Thank you, Chuckie," John whispered in his ear. "That's the nicest bouquet anyone ever gave me."

Chuckie moved on to other patients. When John got up from the wheelchair I ducked into the nearest room. He passed my door and went toward the nursing station.

"How did it work out, John?" the nurse asked.

"I got a red rose in my paper cup," John announced with pride.

Spring

As the season moved on, the flower supply increased and so did Chuckie's group of patients. More and more people began to keep paper cups on their bedside tables in hopes that the little flower boy would leave a blossom.

I was beginning to feel satisfied as I moved through the corridors of Hill Haven, doing small things to make patients' lives pleasant and comfortable. The old depression that used to haunt me all the time faded into the background.

"By the way," my favorite nurse said one day, "you'll be graduating soon, won't you, Sandy?"

"One more month," I sighed. "I can hardly stand any more high school."

"Don't you like school?"

"I don't like being the only one in the crowd who is tied down."

"Are you sure the others are so free?" She looked at me questioningly and then went on. "What are you going to do after you graduate?"

"Find some way to support myself and Chuckie."

"Did you ever think of nursing? You're a natural for it."

"I could never get through the years of training with a baby."

"There are shorter courses, Sandy—two years for some schools. People who really want to get through them do . . . all the time."

"I'll think about it," I promised as I started down the hallway.

My thinking was interrupted by the sounds coming from the sun-room, where Chuckie had gone to give out flowers. In the past this had been a quiet job. Never before had the flower routine made people laugh out loud.

"Hang on . . . one more push." It was the elderly grandfather's voice.

"I'll send him back," another voice said.

What on earth are those people doing with their wheelchairs? I wondered. I tiptoed to the doorway of the sun-room to look.

Grinning broadly, Chuckie was sailing across the room on a round disk of wood with two handles to hang onto and four swivel wheels underneath. When he caught his breath his laughter could be heard throughout the entire nursing home.

John was sitting on the floor with an oilcan, a wrench, a screwdriver, and a pair of pliers.

"Bring it over here, Chuckie," he said. "I'll fix it better."

Chuckie sat down on it and tried to make it go.

Nothing happened. He got off and started to push it across the floor toward John.

"No, not that way. Lie down on it."

Chuckie looked blank.

"Like this," John explained, leaning forward and making swimming motions with his hands.

Chuckie got the idea of lying down on it, but still it wouldn't move.

John went over and showed him how to start it with his hands on the floor. The wheels were so smooth-rolling and balanced that the tiniest start carried Chuckie clear across the room.

"Here now," John said as he finished making some adjustments with his tools and putting oil in a few spots. "This should be fine. Sit down on it and we'll give you some rides."

Chuckie sat down.

"Hold the handles," John cautioned.

Chuckie was off. John's push sent him straight across the sun-room to the grandfather's wheelchair. The old man's push sent Chuckie straight back to John.

Chuckie's cheeks became flushed and his eyes glowed with excitement. I remained out of sight and watched. It went on for a dozen trips across the floor.

"That's all for now, Chuckie," John announced. "Time to rest."

He motioned for Chuckie to scoot over by him. Chuckie, exhausted from laughter and excitement, sat willingly on the floor next to John. Instantly his head was leaning on John and his thumb was in his mouth.

John scooped the tired little boy up in his arms and carried him over to the sun-room couch. He laid Chuckie on the cushions and covered him with a blanket that hung over the couch.

"Watch him while he naps, will you, Mr. Tulio? I have to work now," John said.

Mr. Tulio moved his wheelchair close to the sleeping child. John turned to leave the room.

He turned and left the room so quickly, in fact, that we collided in the doorway. John drew back, surprised and embarrassed.

"Oh . . . hi, Sandy. Sorry. Did I hurt you?"

"No, John. But maybe we'd better get out of the doorway. There's a wheelchair coming."

We stepped back and moved close to the corridor wall.

"What is that marvelous thing that Chuckie's been riding on?" I asked. "Where did it come from?"

"That's just between Chuckie and me," he answered with an air of mystery.

"Did you make it, by any chance?" I asked, continuing to pry a little.

John smiled.

"There were some old walkers being thrown out downstairs, and they had swivel wheels that I couldn't see wasted."

"But how did you come up with the flying disk idea? And how did Chuckie get so lucky?"

"It's just an even exchange."

I looked at him questioningly.

"When someone gives you a big red rose for your paper cup, you give him something in return, don't you?"

I must have looked confused.

"Don't worry about it, Sandy," he said, brushing the whole thing aside. "It's something Chuckie and I understand."

"Okay," I said, feeling put off.

I turned to go into the sun-room to see about Chuckie.

"Sandy," John said. He caught my arm as I turned away. "Please talk to me . . . please?"

The hallway was not exactly the place to talk. I could see that John was wondering where we could be alone. The door to a linen storage room was open nearby. John took my arm and led me into it. Quietly he closed the door and turned to me.

"I just have to talk to you, Sandy."

"All right."

"There's been such an empty spot in my life ever since that day at the beach."

Mine too, I thought.

"Linda didn't even begin to fill it."

Hooray for Linda, I thought.

"I made an ass of myself going with her instead of you on graduation night."

You did, I said to myself, you certainly did.

"But Linda has done me one favor in the time I've spent with her. . . ."

Bighearted Linda. Give her a Brownie point.

"She has made me realize once and for all how much I want you and Chuckie in my life."

I felt suddenly weak. This direct honest admission was something I had dreamed of in crazy moments. But never had I seriously expected to hear the words being said to me.

John's soul was in his eyes as he watched my reaction.

"Do you want me after the way I treated you?" he asked.

"I want you, John. Oh, how I want you!"

We were in each other's arms. It was an achingly tender embrace. Only two people who have been hurt by earlier loves could bring to their first kiss such joy of discovery.

For a moment time stood still . . . until the magic spell was abruptly broken. A flustered maid stood in the doorway expecting to fill her linen cart.

Smiling, we gave her the storeroom and went in to see if Chuckie had awakened.

THE GLOW OF THAT MOMENT CARRIED OVER INTO THE days that followed, even though I didn't know exactly what John had meant when he said he wanted Chuckie and me in his life.

If I judged from his words alone, John could have been saying anything, ranging from "I want to marry you" all the way across the board to "I want to move in with you." My guess was that his words probably meant, "When I'm able to do things responsibly . . . to make our threesome operate like a family . . . then we'll get married." This seemed to fit John's character.

And so I tried to content myself with long hours between our times together. John made it clear that he was not staying away by choice.

"Sandy," he explained, "my life is full of everything except you . . . when all I really want is you. But I'm working so I can eat and I'm going to school so I can have a worthwhile career. I don't see what I can cut out of that schedule for more time with you."

"Just keep telling me this, John, and I'll hang on," I promised.

So he did . . . and I did. I treasured each chance we had to be together. Mostly these times were after the evening shift at Hill Haven when John would stop by for a quick snack. Usually he was too tired to even want to talk very much, so we sat together on the couch and just enjoyed being close.

"Sandy," he said one evening as we sat there drowsily, "what are you going to do after you graduate?"

"I don't know. That one isn't so easy to plan when you have a young son to care for."

"I think you ought to consider some kind of nursing training. You're a natural for it."

"You're the second person to tell me that."

"Would your mother keep baby-sitting if you went on to school?"

"She said she'd continue while I get trained for

some kind of steady work—and that's about all she'll be able to manage. She's not too strong anymore."

"I'll bring you a course catalog from Fairview and you can see what kinds of programs they have."

"This is where I came in," I commented. "You finding me ways to get into classes."

"Well, I like the way you're happy when you're taking a class you enjoy." He grinned. "And I like the idea of having you on campus taking classes that tie in with my paramedical training."

"Okay," I agreed. "Bring me the catalog and I'll study it."

SEVERAL DAYS LATER CHUCKIE AND I WENT OVER TO visit Aunt Mary at Hill Haven. It was late in the afternoon and as we came near the entrance we saw a figure squatting near the bushes. It was John, making notes on a pad and looking thoughtful.

"Writing a book or making out your grocery list?" I asked.

"Making out a list, yes. Groceries, no."

"Okay, tell me."

"The big flower grower in town donated some money to beautify Hill Haven and make it more cheerful. His grandmother is a patient here and he wants to add some life to the place. So they've given me the responsibility of using the money wisely."

"Hey, that's really fun . . . spending someone

else's money to do good things. What are you going to buy?"

"Right now I'm making drawings for the flower grower. He's going to plan for something to be blooming near the building and in the patio all year around."

"Are you going to spend all the money on plants?"

"I'm open to suggestions. Anything in mind?"

"Nope. But I'll think about it while I go and see Aunt Mary."

Chuckie and I went inside. This time he had no flowers with him because it had been too late to stop on the way. His friends greeted him with smiles and tried to hide their disappointment and their empty paper cups.

We stopped to visit with several patients in the sun-room. In my own mind that spot still echoed with the sounds of Chuckie's laughter as he sped across it on his flying disk. It was still bathed in a golden glow from our linen-room kiss.

As I looked at the patients, though, I could see that none of these things lingered with them. The sun-room was like a morgue—dead silent.

That's awful in there, I thought. You can sit and listen to your own heartbeat. Or you can sit and listen to your own breathing. But there's not much else to hear.

"Aunt Mary," I said as we sat visiting, "what would you buy if you had some money to cheer this place up?"

"A canary for the sun-room, Sandy," she said without hesitation. "I've wished so often for a canary here —a beautiful singer that could be heard down the hallways."

Aunt Mary had put her finger on the perfect purchase. I would never have thought of it in a million years, and yet it was so right. I remembered back to my grandmother's canary. On gloomy days that little yellow bird made sunshine of his own by singing his heart out. I hadn't thought about him for a long, long time.

Feeling as if I had just unlocked some hidden treasure, I hurried out to share the exciting idea with John.

"A bird?" he asked, sounding as if he couldn't believe what he had heard. "A bird?"

"Oh, yes. Haven't you ever heard a really good singing canary?"

"No. But it doesn't sound like much of an idea to me, Sandy."

"I think it does. Aunt Mary thinks it does."

"How do you know what Aunt Mary thinks about it?" Suddenly John was angry. "Sandy, did you go blabbing about the money to patients?"

He had managed to pop my balloon. He didn't like the idea. He thought I'd been blabbing to everyone. Why had he asked me if he wasn't going to pay any attention to what I suggested?

I felt like walking away and telling him to forget it, to leave me out of the planning. But the canary bird was such a good idea that I couldn't let it get lost.

"I didn't blab," I said, defending myself. "I didn't even tell Aunt Mary there was any money. I only asked what she would do if she were going to brighten things up around here. And I think her idea is wonderful!"

"I think it sounds kind of dumb."

"Maybe that's because you aren't a little old lady. Or maybe it's because you never knew a canary. Personally I think the idea is perfect."

"Okay, little old lady," John agreed with a resigned air, "you want a canary for the sun-room, we buy a canary."

"Just like that?" I asked. "No more objections?"

"Who's going to argue with little old ladies about canary birds?" John answered. "You go and price them and I'll get the purchase order."

That's really something, I thought to myself as Chuckie and I walked home later. He agreed to a bird only because I wanted it.

WE MOVED ALONG THE ROWS OF CANARY CAGES IN THE pet store, looking over possible candidates.

"What on earth do you look for when you're buying a canary?" John asked.

"Their song, I guess . . . and then their coloring."

"Suppose you buy one and he refuses to sing?" John asked, doubtfully studying his purchase order.

"You only buy one that comes with a written guarantee that he'll sing or they'll replace him."

"There's one singing over there," he said.

I looked where he was pointing. It was a carrot-colored bird, singing his heart out. I went closer to admire him and fell in love with him instantly. Instead of the sleek head of ordinary canaries, he had bangs coming down on his forehead, giving him a tousled, unkempt look. A very casual-looking bird . . . until you listened to his song . . . and then he became a master musician.

I stood there, glued to the floor in front of his cage.

"Come on, Sandy, let's look at the others. If Aunt Mary is dreaming of an old-fashioned canary like grandma used to have, she wouldn't even recognize this shaggy bird as a canary."

"Aw, he's so cute."

"Come on, let's tend to business. We're buying an old-fashioned yellow canary bird for a lot of old-fashioned people in a nursing home, remember?"

"I love this one."

"I know. But he has to please people who grew up with yellow canaries."

Reluctantly I moved on, the song of that tousle-headed orange bird echoing in my head.

"Here's a yellow one singing," John called from the end of the row. "He's from Holland, it says. See what you think of him."

"He looks good and sounds good," I agreed as I studied him. "He would fit in nicely, I think."

"Okay, pick a cage you like for him."

"Do we need one with a stand?"

"No stand, Sandy. That's too risky with unsteady

patients. I'm going to get a ceiling hook and a long brass chain and let the cage swing from it. No one will knock it over that way, and the floor under it can be cleaned easily."

"Smart idea," I said as I moved along the row of cages. "Look, how about this cage? It's sort of like an old-fashioned cottage."

"They'd like it," he agreed.

So we bought all the supplies that go along with a bird . . . and the cage . . . and the yellow canary . . . and started for the door.

"Hold it just a minute, John. Let me take one last look at that shaggy fellow I like."

John stood there patiently leaning on the counter while I went back for a final look and listen.

"I have to remember that song for dreary days at home," I explained as I picked up our packages and held the door open for John to come through with the cage and the bird.

"Still think it's a dumb idea?" I asked.

"I could learn to like him, I think."

"Good man."

As I OPENED THE FRONT DOOR OF HILL HAVEN A FEW days later the place was flooded with canary song. It was almost as if overnight they had painted the walls with sunshine.

Chuckie and I approached the sun-room expecting

to see a group of wheelchairs clustered around the canary's cage. The bird was, after all, the only new action in the whole nursing home.

To my surprise, the canary was singing only to himself. The wheelchairs were lined up facing the patio windows.

A fine thing, I thought. We go through all that hassle to buy him, and they all turn their backs on him.

Then I saw one patient nudge another and point to the patio. Immediately all the patients in the lineup were alerted. I moved over behind their chairs to see what the show was.

John had just appeared outside the windows, pushing a wheelbarrow loaded with plants. He lifted each pot with care and set it on the patio cement. Again and again he repeated the process until he had a great mass of plants in front of the windows.

One of the patients tapped on the window. John glanced up and smiled at her. At the same time he noticed me and came to the doorway.

"Why don't you get Chuckie's flying disk from the closet and let him play with it out here while you give me some opinions on the planting?"

I nodded and led Chuckie to the closet. Together we went out to join John.

"There are some beautiful plants here," I said as I studied the assortment.

"That's true," John agreed. "There's a lot of money sitting around in these pots. And this isn't all of them, either."

"Where could you possibly plant more than these?" I wondered.

"There's no room here, certainly," John said. "But I've planned an area in the back to be the patients' cutting gardens. I'm planting it with all the kinds of flowers that people like to pick. In that garden patients or nurses can pick anything they want whenever they want it."

"What a beautiful idea," I said.

John smiled. "So they will always have flowers for their paper cups," he explained.

THE BEAUTIFICATION JOB MADE A DIFFERENCE IN HILL Haven. It made an even greater difference in John. Each day he seemed a little more at peace with himself and a little more certain of his role in the medical world.

My own future was still a blur. John's words had become part of my everyday thinking—*I know now how much I want you and Chuckie in my life*—but John and I had never had another moment of real closeness. Mostly we had worked together on bird-buying and landscaping and making things more pleasant for sick people. I still didn't know what kind of commitment went with his statement.

"Here's the catalog from Fairview," John said with a casual air when he stopped at my apartment one Saturday in May. "You could get started in summer session."

I glanced up in surprise.

"How come you're so anxious to get me educated?" I asked suspiciously.

"You're a natural for nursing, Sandy. You get happy when you're helping patients. And I like you happy."

I smiled, willing to accept that explanation.

"And when you're trained," he continued, "maybe we can settle in some community . . . maybe a beach town . . . that needs a medical team to assist their overworked doctor. That would be a good life for Chuckie, don't you think?"

I stood there, speechless. I never dreamed John had long-range plans for the three of us.

John searched my eyes for some sort of reaction.

"Wouldn't you like that kind of marriage, Sandy?"

Suddenly my knees became rubbery. I plopped down on the nearby couch. Finally I found some words.

"You never even mentioned marriage before, John. And now out of a clear blue sky you're asking me what *kind* of marriage I'd like."

"I . . . thought you knew," he answered, fumbling for words. "I was sure you understood."

"I was afraid to jump to any conclusions, John. 'I want you and Chuckie in my life' was what you said. To some guys this means 'I'll move in with you and we'll stay together as long as it's fun.' "

John looked hurt.

"That's not what Chuckie needs," he said, glancing over at the crib. "And that's not what you need,

Sandy. You've been that route before—having some-one take off when the responsibilities begin. That's not what I'm offering you."

He sat down and pulled me close. In his arms I felt safe and protected in a way I had never dreamed possible.

"We'll share the fun and the frustrations and the work and the decisions and the rewards. We'll be a team, Sandy."

He was saying all the things that never were said before my first marriage. And he was forgetting all the things I had considered so romantic—which later turned out to be so empty. Here was a man offering to open his life and take me into it as a full partner.

"I'll work, John," I said as I gave him an extra hug. "I'll learn my nursing lessons so well that you'll be proud to have me on your team. I'll be the best nurse you could have found."

"Just be you, Sandy," he said as he kissed the top of my head. "I'm marrying you, not some nurse."

THE SCHOOL YEAR MOVED ON. SENIOR ACTIVITIES SIG-naled the approach of graduation. And all the while I managed to be out of step with the crowd.

I didn't even mention the senior prom to John be-cause I couldn't see spending so much money on one evening.

At the senior picnic, while everyone was swim-ming or working on their suntans, I cut out from the group and followed a path through the trees to be by myself near the creek.

While the class gathered for the baccalaureate service at one church, I went alone to another and silently prayed for help in raising Chuckie and for a real understanding of John's needs.

And while other seniors seemed to consider graduation a high point of their lives, I only viewed it as a passport to the nursing program I had enrolled in at Fairview.

"We really should do things up right on graduation night," John said one evening. "In fact, since I blew it for both of us on my own graduation night, this time we should do things doubly right."

I felt doubtful. There really wasn't much to do.

"How do you want to celebrate?" he asked.

"Why don't you plan it?" I suggested. "There are several parties that night. Do whatever you want about them. I'll just take care of getting Mom to baby-sit for the evening."

With that I left the graduation night plans in John's hands. I would worry instead about the possibility of tripping as I walked across to receive my diploma.

AS THE MUSIC BEGAN AND THE PROCESSION STARTED TO move, I spotted John and Chuckie and Mom seated on the aisle I was coming down.

Chuckie was twisted around, peeking over his

grandma's shoulder, apparently looking for me. He discovered me in the line of graduates just as I neared his row. He reached out as I passed and I touched his hand. Then I put my finger to my lips to tell him to keep quiet.

He did . . . through the long ceremony . . . except for the one moment when they read out my name and I walked over to receive my diploma. Loud and clear his voice rang out.

"Mamma. There's Mamma."

A ripple of laughter passed over the audience. I couldn't hide my smile. The audience broke into applause. Then it spread to the people on the stage. It was as if the whole community was heaving one big sigh of relief that I had made it—or rather that Mom and Chuckie and I had made it together.

As we marched back up the aisle, fully graduated, Chuckie was reaching out to me with both arms. I couldn't resist him. Lifting him up, I carried him out to the lobby. There we waited for Mom and John.

As we stood there, many people—some strangers, even—came along and congratulated me, or patted Chuckie, or just smiled. The same community that for months had been completely impersonal about my very personal struggle, suddenly was paying attention.

Where were they all when I really needed help? I thought bitterly. But as I listened to their words of congratulations I sensed their surprise. They simply had not known of the struggle that had gone on right under their noses.

"They're proud of you, Sandy," John observed as he stood by me in the lobby. "And so am I," he added.

"That's what really matters," I said as he steered the three of us toward the exit.

"WE'LL HAVE TO STOP AT MY PLACE AND PICK UP YOUR graduation present," John announced as he started his engine. "It wouldn't fit in my pocket."

"Oh?" I answered, feeling warm inside at the idea of John's having picked out a gift for me.

He glanced over at me with a sly grin—like a little boy who had done something he was secretly proud of, but hoped other people would praise him for too.

"Want to give me any clues?" I asked as we drove along.

"Nope."

We stopped in front of his rooming house and John turned to the back seat where Mom was holding Chuckie on her lap.

"We'll be down in just a minute. Do you mind waiting? I need Sandy to help with the gift."

"Wha—at?" I asked.

John was not in a talking mood. He simply opened the car door and motioned for me to come with him. Obediently I followed him up to the second floor. He unlocked the door and led the way into his room, lighted only by a street lamp. Closing the door softly behind us, John turned and took me in his arms.

"Happy graduation, Sandy. I had to have you to myself for a moment before we start partying."

As he held me close I began to melt inside.

"You know . . ." I whispered, "maybe I just graduated from school, but in your arms I'm decidedly not a schoolgirl."

"I'm way beyond schoolgirls and game-playing," John whispered.

After a moment—with what seemed to be considerable effort on his part—John pulled away. He held me at arm's length for a moment, studied my face in the dim light from the street lamp, and smoothed my hair with both of his hands.

"I want tonight to be the happiest time you've ever had so far in your life, Sandy. Even happier days might come, but let's start with tonight."

"Okay," I agreed.

"Want your present?"

"I have it. Your love is my present."

"That's true. But I bought you something too."

He flipped the light switch and there was my gift on the table—an antique brass birdcage . . . and, sleeping inside the cage, the tousle-headed orange canary I had admired in the pet shop.

The bird blinked his eyes as he tried to get used to the sudden brightness that had broken into his night's sleep. Then he burst into song, that same song that had caught and held me in the store.

"Like him?" John asked.

"Like him! That only half says it."

I peered into the cage, enchanted. The shaggy bird

stared right back at me with his bright, beady eyes.

"By the way, your mother and Chuckie are waiting," John reminded me as I started a private conversation with my new pet. "Here, you take these and I'll carry the cage."

He gathered up the birdseed, gravel, bath, and cage papers and handed them to me. Lifting the birdcage in one hand, he steered me toward the door. As he turned off the light switch he lightly brushed my cheek with a kiss.

"I wish you could stay all night," he whispered.

"So do I," I whispered back.

We started down the narrow stairway.

"John, you shouldn't have gotten yourself tied up with a girl who has built-in responsibilities," I suggested, feeling wistful and a little guilty.

"I tried the other kind and couldn't stand it, remember? And besides, I don't call it 'being tied up' when I willingly go into partnership with someone I choose."

"You're already assembling quite a permanent household here with this new addition," I said as I took a quick look into the brass cage.

"Well," he said very slowly, "there's something about the song of that shaggy canary . . ."

AFTER A SHORT STOP AT MY APARTMENT TO GET Chuckie and my new canary settled with Grandma,

John and I were off again—for partying, as he called it.

"Be young and carefree tonight," my mother called as we went down the front steps. "Try to feel like a graduating senior for a few hours, honey."

We waved and thanked her.

"I don't think I want to feel like a graduating senior," I confided to John when we were settled in the car. "Grad night is game night to the people I know."

John looked over at me and nodded his head knowingly. Apparently the memory of his own graduation night with Linda was still painfully fresh in his mind.

"Before we try these parties would you mind doing one thing just for me, Sandy?" John asked as he started the engine.

"I'm sure I won't. What is it?"

"I've told the Strombergs about you, and they know you're graduating tonight. Could we go out there and let them meet you? Would you mind . . . really?"

"Of course I wouldn't mind."

"You may be in a hurry to get to the graduation parties," he argued.

"The parties are unimportant," I reassured him. "They are just something that people do on graduation night."

John still looked doubtful.

"I *want* to meet the Strombergs," I said, trying to be as convincing as possible. "I really do. So could we please go and see them? Now?"

Looking much relieved, John pulled out from the curb and headed north.

"They are kind of old-fashioned, Sandy. They have lived here twenty-five years, but they still have some old-country ways."

"Since you like them, John, I'll like them. Quit worrying."

Nevertheless, John was nervous. It was clear that our meeting was a matter of great importance to him.

THE STROMBERGS LIVED IN A NEAT LITTLE HOUSE WITH a carefully tended garden at the far end of town. At first glance I was reminded of their beach cottage.

"Mr. Stromberg built the beach cottage and this one too," John explained, as if he had read my thoughts. "He's a carpenter."

The door opened wide as we neared it, and Mrs. Stromberg stood ready to embrace John.

"My boy," she whispered as she hugged him. Then she turned and took both of my hands in hers. "And this is Sandy. Welcome to our home."

Mr. Stromberg was standing close by, ready to continue with the greetings. He led us into a cozy living room filled with family memories.

There were pictures of John with Paul at every age. John and Paul in the redwoods, John and Paul on a mountain peak, by a river, at a lake, in school, at the beach, inside car hoods, everywhere. Suddenly I knew that John's life was permanently interwoven with the Strombergs'. He was indeed a part of their family—all they had left, in fact. No wonder it had mattered so much to him whether or not I wanted to come.

"Let me fix some coffee," Mrs. Stromberg said as she moved toward the kitchen.

"Oh, no, please, Aunt Britt," John said. "Don't bother tonight. We can only stay a minute. It's graduation night, you know, and Sandy has been invited to several parties. But we'll come back another time for coffee."

I could sense the deep disappointment Mrs. Stromberg was feeling. Serving coffee to guests was an old Swedish custom, and she was being deprived of the chance to honor her visitors.

"Let's be late to the parties and have some coffee with the Strombergs," I suggested. "I'd like to."

John agreed with enormous relief. Immediately he and Mr. Stromberg became lost in conversation. I went to the kitchen to help Mrs. Stromberg.

She was busily arranging a tray of fancy Swedish cookies which obviously had been fresh baked for this occasion. As she moved comfortably about the kitchen I noticed there were tears in her eyes. Finally she looked up.

"Sandy, you have no idea how long and hard I've prayed for you."

"For me?" I asked in surprise.

"For you! Ever since Paul died, John has been at loose ends. No one besides Paul had ever been close to him, close enough to share his thoughts and feelings. He wasn't likely to form another close friendship with a young man at this age, and so I knew he was going to have to be lonely until a young woman came along to fill the emptiness . . . one who would understand him and share his life . . . a partner, really—not a useless and demanding ornament."

She looked over her shoulder to be sure John wasn't listening. "Like that Linda," she whispered.

I grinned. I knew just what she meant.

"You're right for John, Sandy. That's been clear to me for a long time. He changed when you came into his life—and I certainly hope you're there to stay."

"So do I," I whispered as I picked up the cookie tray and followed Mrs. Stromberg into the living room.

"These are wonderful cookies," I said as we visited over the steaming strong coffee she had served in tiny coffee cups.

"I'll give you the cookie recipe," Mrs. Stromberg said in a motherly way. "John has always liked them."

"Chuckie would too," John added. "He's a real cookie freak."

The Strombergs then wanted to see the picture of Chuckie that I carried in my wallet. They admired him and said they hoped we'd bring him over to visit soon.

The evening could have gone on for hours with the pleasant conversation and genuine interest that the Strombergs were feeling, but eventually John looked at his watch and stood up to leave.

Mrs. Stromberg put an arm around my shoulder.

"I feel so much better now that my prayers have been answered," she whispered in my ear. "Thank you for coming to meet us, dear."

"Thank *you,*" I answered.

"You were wonderful," John said as we drove away from the cottage.

"I didn't do anything."

"That's why you were so wonderful. Your warmth and courtesy just came naturally. Mrs. Stromberg had dreamed for days of entertaining you. You sensed it and stayed to visit."

"That wasn't hard, John. I felt as if I were visiting your family."

"They are."

We drove on in silence.

"WHAT'S THE ADDRESS OF THAT FIRST PARTY—THE ONE on Crocker Street?" John asked, finally breaking the silence.

"It's 1302. Joan Henry's."

"It must be the green house on the left. There are plenty of people there, judging from the cars parked outside."

That was the understatement of the year. When some guest or other opened the front door for us, we could only wonder where they were going to put two more bodies. All available sitting, standing, and breathing space was fully occupied.

"Make yourselves at home," the girl said. "Joan's lost . . . somewhere in this mess. But the food is in that direction." She pointed us toward a far-off corner just before she, too, was swallowed up by the crowd.

It was like making our way through a rush-hour bus. After we had pushed forward about ten feet John tugged on my hand.

"This is supposed to be fun?" he whispered.

I shrugged my shoulders. The food was still half a room away in spite of all our efforts.

"Want to leave?" I asked.

"Definitely!"

John took my hand and ran interference for me as we headed back the way we had come. Joan was near her front door this time.

"Did you two get enough to eat?" she asked.

"Oh, yes. Thanks for inviting us, Joan."

"I'm so glad you could come."

We were free again. Fresh air to breathe and enough quiet to hear ourselves speaking.

"Whew, that's what I call partying," John said. "I think I'm too old for it."

"I can't take it either," I agreed. "After the Strombergs it all seemed like a set of plastic people in a game."

"What about the other two parties?" John asked as we sat in the car trying to recover from Joan's.

"Well, I would guess that Harriet's crowd won't care whether or not we get there because they will all be stoned. And Melanie's crowd will already be pretty far gone because they like their booze early."

"So why don't we forget the parties and just be us?" John suggested.

I nodded in agreement.

"We did give it a good try, didn't we? Celebrating, I mean," John asked as we drove away. "I feel a little guilty dropping it all in the middle."

"We gave it all the tries I want," I answered.

"Any place else you'd like to go instead?"

"Not really. I'm enjoying being with you . . . somewhere . . . anywhere."

John looked over and smiled. With his right arm he pulled me closer to him.

"We don't have Chuckie between us tonight, you know. You don't have to hold a seat for him."

"He could have the seat by the window even if he were here," I said. "I'll take the place by the man."

"Good girl," John said, patting my knee.

THE CITY TRAFFIC HAD THINNED OUT BY THE TIME WE reached the coast highway. The beauty of the June night suddenly unfolded before us. The air was warm and the moon was full. Whenever we could catch a glimpse of the ocean, the moonlight made the white-caps glisten like white frosting on the dark waves.

"Why don't we stop somewhere and get a real view of the ocean?" I suggested. "I've never seen such a beautiful night."

"Want to go to our own beach and enjoy it down near the water?" John asked.

But he had second thoughts on his suggestion. "That wouldn't work. You have on your graduation outfit and the sand could wreck your shoes." He shrugged his shoulders as if to close the subject.

"Unless maybe you want to leave your shoes in the car." He looked at me questioningly.

"That would work," he added. "Barefoot would be okay. It's a sandy path as soon as we get out of the parking circle."

He nodded to himself. "The parking area isn't very rocky, either," he said as a final clincher.

I looked at him and laughed.

John, realizing how much of a one-man conversation he had been carrying on, laughed too.

"Yes or no. Do you want to go to our beach?" he asked very simply.

"Of course," I answered. "I was just waiting until you had yourself convinced."

ALTHOUGH THERE WERE SCATTERED LIGHTS IN THE COTtages along the road, the parking circle was very dark. I stepped barefoot out onto the dirt and landed on a sharp rock.

"Ouch."

"It becomes sandy just as soon as we get off the road," John reassured me. "This is the only rough part."

"You going to join me barefoot?" I asked.

John put his shoes and socks in the car and rolled his pants legs up.

"We're certainly a pair of 'be-yourselfers' for graduation night, aren't we?" I said, laughing.

"Here, Sandy, give me your hand on this dark path. I know it by heart."

For an instant I was back on that first visit to this beach, following an unhappy young man down a dark path.

John's voice brought me back to graduation night. It was the same dark trail and we were the same two people. Or were we?

"Sandy?" John said as if he might have tried several times before I heard him. He squeezed my hand.

"H'mm?"

"What did Aunt Britt tell you in the kitchen?"

"Why?"

"I just wondered."

"She said she was glad you had found me."

"That's not all."

"How do you know?"

"Because that wouldn't make Aunt Britt cry, and she had tears in her eyes when she came into the living room."

"She said you had been lonely since Paul's death."

"And . . . ?"

"That's about it."

"What did she really say, Sandy?"

"That she had prayed for me to come along and fill the emptiness in your life!"

John was silent for a long time.

"I certainly wouldn't want to tamper with Aunt Britt's prayers," he said finally. And he was silent again.

We strolled hand in hand to the water's edge.

"Do you want to start thinking about when?" John asked, breaking a long comfortable silence.

"When what?"

"When we can get married, of course."

"John," I said, turning him toward me so I could look straight into his eyes. "Are you certain that marriage is what you want? Am I really the one for you? And most of all, are you doubly sure you want to be a bridegroom and a father all on the same day?"

"I know you have reason to doubt it, Sandy. I remember—with some embarrassment—that when we first met I made it clear our friendship was not to lead to anything that would tie me down."

"That's why I'm asking."

"I was hurt and confused then, Sandy. By Paul's death . . . and Linda's crazy games . . . and not knowing what to do with my life after the service."

He turned away for a moment, looking up toward the Stromberg cottage.

"You were hurting too," he reminded me.

"I know."

"We've been changing," John said.

He studied my face in the moonlight.

"Now that you're going into nursing we're both moving toward the same kind of life. . . . We both want Chuckie. . . . I have enough money from my

GI benefits and my job for us to get along . . . so what good reason can there be for putting off becoming a family?"

"We're young?" I said, wondering if that was a good reason.

"It's right for us, Sandy," John said. "I've known it for a long time."

He put his arms around me and held me close.

"It's gotten so that I'm so lonely when I'm away from you and Chuckie I can't study. All I can think of is being with you."

"It's not so easy to study around Chuckie," I pointed out.

"That's a hazard I'm willing to face. I'd rather work on the family-type problems than the problems we would have apart."

He looked at me questioningly. "So when shall we get married, Sandy?"

"Let's figure. Fairview summer session begins in ten days. How about our getting enrolled and started in classes and then having our wedding on the second Saturday?" I suggested.

". . . and the Nolans had a whole day's honeymoon," John said with a grin.

When he kissed me again I knew that for both of us three weeks was too far away.

"Okay, how about a week from tomorrow?" I asked.

"I'll take it!" John said.

Summer

WE AGREED ON A SIMPLE FAMILY WEDDING. WE WANTED to enjoy the occasion.

Mrs. Stromberg, knowing that my mother had only a small apartment, offered her home for the ceremony and wedding supper. Since this sounded fine to us, she and Mom got together on plans.

"Could it possibly be a Swedish smorgasbord supper?" I asked Mrs. Stromberg.

"Of course," she agreed with delight. "If you like, I'll even use our traditional table decorations that came with us from Sweden."

The rest of the wedding preparations were simple. Besides the Strombergs and my mother, we invited only Edith and Georgie Klopman and Aunt Mary Miller, who could come in a wheelchair.

I bought a blue dress I would enjoy wearing after the wedding. Chuckie could wear the red outfit I had made in class. We were all fixed up with no fuss at all.

"Would you like some flowers?" John asked.

"I really would like a bouquet of blue cornflowers

and forget-me-nots picked from the Strombergs' garden. Do you think they would mind?"

"I think they'll be pleased," John said. "I'll arrange for your bouquet and have it ready."

AND SO OUR WEDDING DAY ARRIVED AND NO ONE WAS tired or flustered or bothered with last-minute details. It was a happy day.

John came for us at three o'clock. He had with him a lovely old-fashioned bouquet, more beautiful than I had expected and yet just what I wanted. Mrs. Stromberg and he had prepared it together that morning.

There was no chance to be alone before loading Chuckie and Grandma into the back seat and heading for the Strombergs'. But I felt John's touch, unnoticed in the back seat, a silent message from the bridegroom.

I've never really been married before, I thought to myself. There should be some other name for what I had before—it was legal but it was nothing.

"I'm not even scared," I whispered to John. "Just happy."

"That's what you're supposed to be."

"Lots of brides are scared—of the ceremony, of the uncertainty of the future, of the rightness of their decision."

"We'll muddle through our problems and find some

fun in living, Sandy. It's right, what we're doing. I feel sure of it."

The Strombergs' long-time Lutheran minister was already in the living room when we arrived. After introductions and greetings we went into another room to discuss with him the vows we had chosen for the ceremony.

In another ten minutes John and I were standing in front of a tall antique Swedish candelabrum that held five large glowing candles. We repeated our vows before the guests.

> "I, Sandra Martin, take you, John Nolan, to be my husband, and these things I promise you: I will be faithful to you and honest with you. I will respect, trust, help, and care for you. I will share my life with you. I will try to better understand ourselves, the world, and God—with you. And these things I will do through the best and the worst of what is to come . . . as long as we live."

John, in his turn, repeated the same vows. Then he held out his hand for Chuckie to come to him. With Chuckie at his side John made the rest of his promises.

> "I, John Nolan, take you, Charles, to be my son, and these things I promise you: I will love you, care for you, and provide for you. I will help you explore the world around you. I will help you understand and appreciate the people in your life. And—along with your mother—I will try to create a climate in our home where we can share our joys

and problems and respect each other as individuals."

John dropped Chuckie's hand and ended the ceremony with a kiss for the bride. We were man and wife . . . and son!

IMMEDIATELY THE SMORGASBORD PREPARATIONS BEGAN.

"Sandy," my mother called from the kitchen, "shall we let Chuckie and Georgie eat now so they can play while the rest of us enjoy our supper?"

"Sure, Mom. I'll be right in."

"You certainly won't," came back the reply from the kitchen. "You're the bride. I guess we're able to feed a couple of little boys."

John and I sat down and visited with Aunt Mary and Mrs. Klopman and Mr. Stromberg. Before long two little boys emerged from the kitchen, flashing big smiles and guarding a generous supply of Swedish cookies.

"You boys could eat your cookies in the garden," I suggested. "They'll make a lot of crumbs on Mrs. Stromberg's carpet if you eat them here."

The idea appealed to the boys and they went happily into the yard. I relaxed and settled back to wait for Mrs. Stromberg's beautiful wedding supper.

"It's all been perfect," I told her as she brought in the last of the fancy foods. "And I loved having the antique candelabrum with the lighted candles for our ceremony."

"It's yours, Sandy."

"Wha—a—at?"

"It's your wedding gift. John has always admired it, so we decided you two should have it for your home. It belonged to my great-grandmother in Sweden, you know."

I went over and rubbed it lovingly. John had heard the news from across the room and came over too.

"Aunt Britt, are you sure you can part with it?" he asked.

"I'm not really parting with it. I feel as if it's still in the family. This way I know that it will be carried on through more generations."

"Thank you for everything," I said as I gave her a hug.

"Let's share our smorgasbord now," Mrs. Stromberg said, patting my cheek as she moved away. "But first, a prayer for the bride and groom."

The minister offered a prayer for our new home, Mrs. Stromberg lighted the candles on the table, and our wedding supper was under way.

"Isn't it nice that Georgie and Chuckie can play happily by themselves," my mother commented as we served up our plates. "The enclosed garden here is so safe and pleasant."

As the supper progressed, John squeezed my hand under the table. It was a see-you-later message. We still had a long way to go before we could be completely alone. After the supper we had to take

Chuckie to his grandma's apartment, where he would sleep for two nights. We were going to have a mini-honeymoon before Fairview summer session started.

"THIS IS A LOVELY MEAL," AUNT MARY SAID TO MRS. Stromberg. "I'm afraid you're spoiling me. Hill Haven food will look even worse after this feast."

"When we're settled, may I get some of these recipes?" I asked.

Mrs. Stromberg nodded to me and smiled appreciatively at all her guests. "I have never prepared a meal with more joy," she replied.

A mellowness was settling over the crowd and I had the feeling that no one but John and I cared if they ever moved again.

Just at that moment Georgie came running in from the garden.

"Chuckie's crying," he announced.

"Did you do anything to make him cry?" Mrs. Klopman asked.

Georgie shook his head. "He fell down the steps."

"Maybe I'd better go see about it," John said quietly. "You finish your dessert, Sandy."

In seconds Georgie was back tugging at my arm. "John says come!"

I dashed out the door and found John kneeling over a bleeding child.

"Put some ice cubes in a plastic bag," John said, "while I stop this bleeding from his forehead. And bring a box of tissues," he called. I was already half-way to the kitchen.

"What's happened?" everyone asked.

"He just cut his forehead," I said, trying to sound very calm. My heart was racing and fear was making my throat feel tight. "It will be all right, I'm sure," I added, hoping they would not get excited. But of course they did.

Mrs. Stromberg handed me a pile of clean towels. My mother prepared a bigger and better ice pack. I hurried back to John and Chuckie.

"I've got the bleeding stopped," he said, "but there's a nasty gash that probably should have stitches."

Carefully he lifted the compress of tissues to show me the wound underneath. I felt suddenly ill. I could feel myself getting faint.

"Sit down on the step here, Sandy, and put your head between your knees," John ordered. "You'll be okay in a minute."

He was right. In seconds I was feeling better. Chuckie doesn't need a fainting mother, I told myself, and John doesn't need a frail assistant.

"You okay?" John asked. "I couldn't help much because I didn't dare take the pressure off this compress."

"I'm fine," I said. "But what do you think about Chuckie?"

"We should get him to the emergency room," he answered.

Gently John started to lift Chuckie. The instant he did Chuckie let out a sharp cry.

"Arm," he whimpered. "Arm . . . arm."

Our attention had been focused entirely on the bloody forehead gash. We hadn't even looked at the rest of the child. It didn't take an expert to tell that the forearm was broken. It was out of shape and swelling fast.

"Get me a magazine and a dish towel," John ordered. Immediately the ladies appeared with them.

"We're going to rest your arm inside this magazine, Chuckie, and then put it in this sling," John explained quietly as if Chuckie would understand just what he was talking about.

Chuckie gulped back more tears. John talked steadily as he tied the sling around Chuckie's neck.

"There now, it will still hurt, but the magazine will keep it from flopping around and getting the bones more out of line."

Chuckie continued to whimper, but John's calm talking kept him from panic.

"Now, Sandy, set the ice pack carefully inside the sling next to his arm," John said. "It will lessen the pain and help to keep the swelling down."

"I'd better phone Dr. Klein and see if he can meet us at the emergency room, don't you think?" I asked John.

"Right. You do that now while I load Chuckie into the car."

I rushed in to phone. Everyone else hurried out to

offer kind words as John carried his new son to the car.

"I got Dr. Klein," I called as I ran down the cement garden steps. "He'll meet us there."

Everyone was gathered around the car wishing us well.

"Thank you for everything," I said. "All of you."

"Let us know about Chuckie as soon as you can," they shouted as we drove off.

John looked over at me.

"Happy wedding day, Mrs. Nolan."

I put my hand to my forehead.

"This isn't quite the way I had planned it," I said weakly.

"YOUR NAME, PLEASE?" THE SECRETARY AT THE EMERGENCY room asked.

"Mr. and Mrs. John Nolan," John replied without hesitation.

"I think they'll need the insurance card," I whispered. "Can you get it out of my wallet? I don't want to move Chuckie."

"This says the child is Charles Martin," the lady said doubtfully. "We can't do a thing for the child without his parents' permission."

"I *am* his mother," I said with indignation.

"And I just married his mother," John added, "an hour ago."

"Oh . . ." the secretary murmured, changing her attitude completely. "Happy honeymoon."

Quickly she completed the forms.

"Would you lay him on the table in the first room on the left, please?" she asked. "Dr. Klein is coming right down."

"They'll fix up your arm and your head here," John said to Chuckie. "It's a hospital."

Chuckie looked frightened. John gave him an encouraging smile. Just then Dr. Klein came in.

"Hi, Sandy," he said while he was patting Chuckie.

"Hello, Dr. Klein. This is my husband, John."

Dr. Klein flashed John a hostile look and immediately turned his attention back to Chuckie. I had the feeling that he hated John without even knowing him.

"You've been away for a while, haven't you?" he said without looking up. "Like ever since Sandy was two months pregnant."

"No, Dr. Klein, you have the wrong man," I hurried to explain. "John and I were married only an hour ago. He's Chuckie's new father—a real father this time."

"Sorry about that mistake," Dr. Klein said, looking up only briefly. "I saw Sandy through that long bitter pregnancy and lonely birth, and I can't forgive the selfish kid who could treat her that way."

With that Dr. Klein turned his full attention to Chuckie's problems. "Would you stand on the other side of the table, Sandy, and hold his good arm? He'll be happier with you close, I think."

I moved over near Chuckie and held his hand.

"You're not the fainting type of mother, are you?" Dr. Klein asked casually.

"Not a bit," I assured him. John winked at me.

"We're going to take pictures of your arm and head," Dr. Klein said to Chuckie. "And we'll let you ride on the rolling table into the other room where the camera is. Okay?"

Chuckie nodded.

"We'll come back to your mommy very soon," we heard him explaining to Chuckie as they moved down to X-ray.

"You can wait in this other room," the nurse said. "There are comfortable chairs and some magazines. We'll call you as soon as they are back."

John and I settled down on a couch.

"How are you doing, Mrs. Nolan?" he asked as he put his arm around my shoulders.

"Badly, thanks," I answered, leaning on him. "I have the feeling I might fall apart any minute."

"Hang on," he advised. "We'll see him through it okay."

AFTER WHAT SEEMED LIKE A VERY LONG TIME A NURSE came to the counter and softly called, "Mrs. Nolan." There was no response inside me. She came over closer. "Mrs. Nolan? You *are* Mrs. Nolan, aren't you?"

John nudged me and suddenly I came to.

"Oh . . . of course I'm Mrs. Nolan. I'm sorry."

"Dr. Klein would like to talk to you and your husband. Follow me, please."

"I'm sure you already know it's a bad fracture of his forearm, don't you?" Dr. Klein said. "We'll have to put him to sleep to set it. And while he's there we'll clean and suture that forehead gash so it won't leave a permanent scar. You agree to this, don't you?"

"Do whatever you feel is right," I said. And then I remembered that now Chuckie had two people responsible for him. "What do you think, John?"

"I would trust Dr. Klein's judgment," he agreed.

"I'll get him into surgery right now. It will take a while. The nurse will call you when he's in the recovery room. But he'll have to sleep here tonight. Don't worry too much. It's the kind of thing we can fix up."

Feeling the tears starting, I nodded and turned away.

John put an arm around my shoulders. "Thank you, doctor," he said.

I felt numb.

"Come on, Sandy. I have an errand to do while Chuckie's in surgery."

"I couldn't possibly leave, John."

"We can be back in twenty minutes. He'll probably be in there for an hour or two."

"Don't you care what's happening in that surgery room?" I asked with a mixture of hurt and anger. "How could you just walk off and leave a little boy alone?"

"I'm not just walking off and leaving a little boy alone. I'm leaving him in the care of one of the best surgical teams in this city, and I'm leaving him in a room where we are barred from entering anyway."

I didn't answer.

"Come on. We can be back before he has his eyes open."

"I don't see how anything could be so important that you'd have to do it right now," I said. My anger was rising. "Is it that much more important than Chuckie?"

"I think it's important or I wouldn't be doing it," John answered. "Besides, what good are you doing Chuckie by sitting on a couch biting your nails?"

"Maybe more good than you'd be doing running around," I snapped back.

"Are you coming or not, Sandy?"

"No!"

"Well, I'll be back here in twenty minutes."

As I watched John move quickly through the automatic doors and on out to the parking lot my stomach froze into a tight little knot. I felt cold all over. The moment reminded me so much of my earlier situation. At a time of crisis I was sitting alone in a hospital, abandoned by my husband.

I curled up on the couch feeling completely sorry for myself. I guess no one can feel the worry and concern over a child that a mother can, I thought to myself. So here I sit holding a lonely vigil . . . just waiting . . . waiting . . . waiting. I had become a genuine soap-opera heroine.

In the distance, through the haze of my thoughts, I heard the sliding of the automatic doors. Instantly I snapped back to reality. John was striding through the doors.

"Any word yet?" he asked, sitting down by me.

I glanced up at the clock. Although it had seemed like an hour, actually John had been gone only fifteen minutes. It was getting hard to keep thinking of him as the irresponsible villain in the soap opera. In a way maybe I was the one who was acting kind of immature.

John set a brown paper bag on the couch.

"What did you get?" I asked.

"Oh, just something I picked up from work."

"Did you have to do it right now?"

"Yes."

I could see I wasn't going to get any information from him.

"There's a vending machine in the next room," John said. "Do you want some coffee or hot chocolate?"

"No, thanks. I don't think I can swallow."

"Are you that scared about Chuckie, Sandy?"

"Not really, I guess. I just panicked when I felt myself abandoned with responsibilities for a second time in my life."

"Abandoned!" he echoed in amazement. "The last thing you are is abandoned."

Quickly he took me in his arms and held me close.

"I should have remembered how you are about some things. I'm sorry, Sandy. I should have explained more. I was just a little hurt that you didn't trust my judgment enough to go out for a quick errand with me, knowing I'd get us back in time."

"Well," I answered, "I still don't see what could have been so urgent."

John reached over and picked up his paper bag. Without a word he set it on my lap. It weighed almost nothing. An empty paper bag? This is what we were quarreling about?

I opened the top. In the dim light I couldn't tell what, if anything, was inside. Hesitantly I reached in and pulled out a single rosebud. One deep-red rose from Hill Haven's rose garden!

"So Chuckie will have his rose in a paper cup on his table when he wakes up in the morning," John explained.

WHEN FINALLY THE NURSE DID TAKE US INTO THE RECOVERY room for a quick look at Chuckie, I was so unnerved from waiting that I was sure I'd break down. John held my hand and tightened his grip each time he felt me starting to crumble.

Together we carried on a fuzzy little conversation with Chuckie. He wasn't really awake and he wasn't sound asleep. Feeling sure he'd get some sort of message through the fog, we repeated over and over again that he was sleeping in the hospital overnight, and we would come for him in the morning.

He was a battered-looking little person with a big

bandage on his head and a cast on his arm, but Dr. Klein assured us that all was well.

"In fact," he said with an air of finality, "it is now time for you two to go home and start your honeymoon."

We grinned.

"You know," he continued, "I've heard of parents doing a lot of things to get the kids out of the house so they could make love—but this is ridiculous!"

Still laughing at Dr. Klein's candid observation, we detoured past the pediatric ward and left the red rose in a paper cup to be placed on Chuckie's bedside table.

"Be sure and tell him John got the rose for him," I urged the nurse.

"And tell him we'll be here early in the morning to take him home," John added.

As we passed a pay phone I finally remembered that my mother and the Strombergs were anxiously waiting for word on Chuckie's condition. John deposited the money and kept his ear close enough to hear. I called Mrs. Stromberg first.

"Your mother left quite a while ago, dear, but I know she's waiting for your call. How is Chuckie?"

I gave her the details and she felt relieved to know he would be out of the hospital in the morning.

My mother was equally relieved by the news.

"I'm so glad he didn't have a concussion . . . and how are you holding up, dear?"

"I'm fine now, Mom."

"Well, don't worry about things any more tonight.

You two certainly have earned some time to yourselves. Give my love to John."

"Okay, Mom, sleep well. I know you're tired."

I hung up the phone and turned to John.

"Anything else I should attend to?"

"Mrs. Nolan," John said with a knowing sort of smile, "it is now time for us to go home and do what Dr. Klein told us to do."

"It surely must be," I agreed. "We've done everything else."

When we opened the apartment door we were faced with the disorder of my wedding preparations.

"Look at the mess I left for us," I moaned.

"If the apartment is a mess, okay, I can bear it," John said philosophically. "If my wife were a mess, well, that might be harder to take."

I started toward the disorder. John caught my arm and pulled me toward him.

"But . . . since my wife is *not* a mess . . ."

He started to kiss me. I gave him a hold-everything, I'll-be-with-you-in-a-minute kiss. I almost turned back for a second one. Instead, I ducked away and hurried around tidying up the place.

"Sandy, it doesn't matter tonight. Really it doesn't."

"I think it does. I think it matters a lot. I'd like the setting to be nice."

"Sandy . . . the *girl* is nice. Very nice. Come on."

His voice was pleading. I was hurrying.

Reluctantly John started picking up a few scattered pieces of clothing from the floor, the bed, the dresser —and put them in the closet. I gathered up Chuckie's lunch and snack dishes and took them to the sink. The laundry went into the hamper, the towels to the bathroom. And with a final sweep of the hand to straighten up the bedspread, I turned to John.

"Now . . . isn't that better? The honeymoon cottage is ready."

"Uh-huh," he agreed, "and the husband is ready."

This time John held his arms open for me and I was ready. All the crazy mess of the last few hours melted away as he held me close.

"Would you believe," my husband whispered in my ear, "that Mr. and Mrs. John Nolan are alone at last in their own home?"

SOMETIME LATER, WHO KNOWS WHEN . . . TIME DIDN'T matter . . . we lay there dreamily trying to absorb the fact that this was for keeps.

"Do you know what?" I said with surprise as my mind unexpectedly flashed back to our earlier times together.

"What?"

"I still have your graduation present. You didn't get it on graduation night as I had planned."

"That was not one of my better nights, was it?"

"As a matter of fact, I almost burned up your gift, I was so mad."

"Want to try me now? I just graduated from bachelorhood to fatherhood in one quick step. Does that earn me a gift?"

"M'mm . . . I guess so," I agreed.

I hated to break the spell by getting up to get the gift. But we would be together again—for the whole night . . . every night.

"Happy graduation to fatherhood," I said as I laid the carefully wrapped book on John's lap.

He opened the package slowly, as if to make the moment last. When he finally removed the last bit of wrappings from the book of beaches, I could tell he was pleased.

"You know how I feel about beaches, don't you, Sandy? So many turning points in my life have come on a beach . . . with Paul . . . with Chuckie . . . with you."

He began studying the book. On each page one of the world's finest photographers had captured some magic moment on a favorite beach. John turned each page silently.

"I've been to some of these places, Sandy. In the service."

He continued through the book.

"Someday I hope we can be together on a few of these beaches," he added. "Maybe live and work near one of them."

"I'll keep that dream before me when school starts Monday at nine o'clock. And every time after that when the roof seems to be falling in."

SUNDAY SEEMED MILD AFTER SATURDAY. DR. KLEIN phoned at ten o'clock to tell us Chuckie was ready for release. Fifteen minutes later, we found our young son sitting on the lap of a teen-age volunteer, waiting impatiently to go home. Proudly he displayed his cast and head bandage.

John studied the cast with a serious expression. Then he reached in his pocket and pulled out a pen.

"Hold still, Chuckie, this operation won't hurt a bit," he said.

Chuckie looked at John with a mixture of trust and curiosity.

With a few quick strokes of his pen John drew a laughing rabbit's face on the cast. Chuckie looked at it and giggled.

"Mamma too," he said.

John placed the pen in my hand and I went to work drawing a little boy's smiling face. Chuckie watched it all with delight.

"Patti," he said, when I had finished.

"Are you Patti?" I asked the volunteer. She nodded and went to work on her picture.

The nurse came in to check on Chuckie's medications and instructions.

"I guess you're in on this, too, Mrs. Rosen," Patti said.

"All right, I'll be back in a minute," the nurse said as she disappeared through the door. She was back shortly with a jar full of colored felt pens.

"Let's dress this cast up a bit," she said. "Pick a color, Chuckie."

Using the pen of his choice, Mrs. Rosen added a few deft strokes to the design. With four more colors she gave the cast its final touch—a brilliant sunburst design with long streaks of bright color.

Chuckie was dazzled.

"I understand you're a new father, Mr. Nolan," the nurse said as she gathered up the pens.

John nodded.

"We do a big business with new fathers," she continued. "But we're used to sending home three-day-old babies with them. This is something else, sending home year-and-a-half-old children with new fathers."

John gave her a shy smile.

"Lots of luck from here on in," she added. "After a beginning like this the rest may seem easy."

She gave a final smoothing to the new dressing on Chuckie's forehead and patted his cheek. "Are you carrying him, Mr. Nolan?"

John held out his arms. Chuckie drew back.

"It's Mamma today, I guess," she said, handing Chuckie over to me. I wished he had wanted John instead, but that would come with time.

John picked up the bag of medications and the release forms. "Thank you very much," he said.

"I'm glad it wasn't worse," Mrs. Rosen answered. "Now can you two finish your honeymoon?"

"We gave up on that," John said. "School starts for both of us tomorrow."

"Try some little two-hour honeymoons whenever you can sandwich them in," she suggested. "Maybe they'll add up."

With a friendly wave she turned and headed for her nursing station.

We moved toward the elevator without speaking. I noticed John winking at Chuckie. Something passed between the two of them.

Chuckie seemed to be in good spirits. He held up his cast and studied the art work.

"John," he said, pointing to the laughing rabbit. "Mamma," he added, displaying my laughing boy. "Patti . . . and Mrs. Wosen."

"Mrs. *Rosen*," I emphasized, hoping to improve the pronunciation of his *r*'s. I was wasting my breath. Chuckie wasn't listening. He was reaching for the elevator button.

The elevator doors closed behind us and we were alone inside. Chuckie made motor noises as the elevator went down. He made door-opening noises as we stepped out into the first-floor lobby. He made engine sounds as he excitedly spotted John's car parked in the loading zone outside the lobby windows.

SUDDENLY THE SCENE CHANGED. CHUCKIE BECAME VERY upset. He squirmed and wiggled in my arms trying to get down. Not wanting to take any chances with his fresh stitches and his new cast, I tried to hang on to him. He pointed toward the elevator.

"Go upstairs," he whined.

"We're going home, Chuckie. Don't you want to go home?" I asked in surprise.

"No," he answered firmly. "Go upstairs."

"Honey, you don't want to stay in the hospital. You *want* to go home, don't you!" This time it was a statement, not a question.

I was getting frustrated. Here we had abandoned our brief honeymoon plans in order to bring this child home and stay with him. Now he had some weird thing about not going home. He wanted to go back to the pediatric ward.

"Isn't that something?" I said to John with some irritation.

John shook his head as if he had no explanation either. But he was willing to give it a try.

"Chuckie," he started quietly and reasonably, "we're going home to your own bed and your teddy bear and the shaggy canary and all your toys."

"Go upstairs," Chuckie insisted.

John stood there scratching his head. Obviously something was bothering Chuckie. But what?

"John go upstairs," Chuckie pleaded.

"Shall I take him up and see what it's all about?" John asked.

"Okay," I agreed. "You try. I'm not doing so well."

I sat down in a lobby chair. John and Chuckie disappeared behind the closing elevator doors.

I sat there watching the elevators open and close, open and close. People came and people went. I wondered uneasily what scene was taking place upstairs in pediatrics.

After a while I didn't even notice the elevator doors opening and closing. The whole pattern had become so mechanical and monotonous that it hardly registered with me when the elevator door eventually opened and John and Chuckie stepped out.

The picture had changed. The distress was gone from Chuckie's face.

"Hi, Mamma," he said, flashing me a brilliant smile. "Go home now."

In his left hand Chuckie clutched a brown paper bag. He held it up as if it were a full explanation.

"What on earth was the matter?" I whispered to John.

"Guess," he urged.

"I can't," I said. I was feeling limp and nervous.

"Let's let Mamma see," John said to Chuckie.

As he said it, John reached for the bag to show me. In a quick flash I saw it all . . . John coming back . . . a brown paper bag . . .

"Don't tell me," I said. "It's the red rose from his paper cup."

John nodded.

"His 'wose.' "

I smiled at John's imitation of Chuckie's speech.

Suddenly it seemed urgent to get out of there before any other crisis arose. I didn't feel up to much more.

"Come on, you guys, do you think we could go home now?" I pleaded with a sigh.

"Why not?" John said agreeably.

Chuckie had never left John's arms. He permitted

himself to be carried to the curb. When I was seated in the car, John eased him in to the front seat, being careful of the cast and head bandage. Inside the car, Chuckie let out a sigh of relief and contentment.

THERE WAS SOMETHING VERY BIG ABOUT THIS MOMENT. The Nolan family was together at last. We were on our way home. The three of us.

As we left the grounds and joined the westbound traffic we all instinctively turned to get one last glimpse of the hospital.

"And so," John said, "as the noonday sun beat down hotly upon our hero and his bride, they rode off into the west where they were to live happily ever after."

"You're reading the wrong script," I said. "Throw that one away!"

I was still reeling from the complications of the last two days—the last fifteen minutes even. The realities were a little overwhelming.

John glanced over at me.

"What are you thinking, Mrs. Nolan?"

"I'm thinking that it's not all going to be roses . . ."

"Woses," he corrected with a knowing wink.